About the Author

Arianne Richmonde is an American writer and artist who was raised in Europe. She lives in France with her husband and coterie of animals. ***Shards of Glass*** is based on much of her personal experience—she used to be an actress.

As well as **The Pearl Series,** she has written *The Star Trilogy*, and the *USA TODAY* bestselling suspense story, ***Stolen Grace***.

Broken Glass

(The Glass Trilogy #2)

by

ARIANNE

RICHMONDE

Copyright © Arianne Richmonde, 2015.
Print Edition

The right of Arianne Richmonde to be identified as the author of this work has been asserted by her under the Copyright Amendment (Moral Rights) 2000

This book is a work of fiction. Names, places, characters, and incidents are either a product of the author's imagination or are used fictitiously, not factually. Any resemblance to actual events, locales or persons, living or dead, is entirely coincidental.

Cover design and photography © by: Arianne Richmonde
Formatting by: BB eBooks

About Shards of Glass

Broken Glass is the second book in *The Glass Trilogy*. This is not a stand-alone; you need to read **Shards of Glass** first.

Daniel Glass is back. Not only as Janie's director, but as her leading man in the BDSM-themed movie, *The Dark Edge of Love*, the sexiest romance since *Fifty Shades of Grey*.

But Janie can't shake off her obsession that Daniel is still in love with his late wife, the invincible blonde bombshell, Natasha Jürgen. Not only that, but rumor has it he's sleeping with half of Hollywood. Janie is determined to keep Daniel at a comfortable distance, but his insistence, charm, and the power he has over her psyche wins her over. She simply can't resist.

Because of family commitments Janie finds herself in Vegas, with Daniel in pursuit. And just when she finds out that he is not the man she feared he was, a calamity befalls the couple.

Daniel Glass is broken . . .

And everything Janie has come to believe . . .

Is worse than just a lie.

1

WHEN I WOKE UP I had no idea where I was. The last thing I remembered was I'd blacked out, Daniel's sexy voice in my ear, threatening to take me over his knee and spank me and fuck some sense into me.

My head was fuzzy. Where was I? I wasn't at Star's. At Daniel's place? Had he taken me here and done unspeakable things to me? If so, why couldn't I remember? It was night, yet the room was not completely dark. I jerked up from the bed but got myself tangled up; I had an IV in my arm. What the hell had happened?

"Janie." It was Daniel sitting in a shadow. He was thumbing through a book.

"Where am I?"

"In Cedars-Sinai Medical Center. Ssh, just relax, don't exert yourself." He took my hand and squeezed it gently.

"I'm in a *hospital*? Why can't I remember getting here?"

"Because you fainted."

I tried to sit up but then slumped back down into the comfort of the pillows. "What's wrong with me?"

"You're suffering from stubbornness, disobedience, and willfulness." He said this deadpan, no trace of a smile.

I stifled a giggle. "Seriously, Daniel, why am I here?"

"You're anemic. They gave you a drip to bring your iron levels up. You've not been eating your spinach, obviously. I should have known—so slim and pale—you need to eat more, Janie, and take care of yourself better. Have you been feeling dizzy, your heartbeat fast or irregular, shortness of breath, cognitive problems, and so on?" He sounded like a doctor, and his expression was deadly serious. All he needed was a clipboard and a white coat.

I cocked a knowing smile. "All of the above."

2

"Shit."

"Definitely cognitive problems; definitely lack of reasoning and rational thought."

"Really?" he said. He didn't catch my irony. Too busy playing doctor.

"If I'd been thinking straight," I told him, "I never would have kissed you at that meeting, and I *certainly* wouldn't even be *contemplating* doing *The Dark Edge of Love* with you, especially now that you're offering yourself up as my leading man."

He tried to contain a smile. "So you *will* work with me again?"

"I didn't say that."

"Well, your wicked sense of humor has returned, Janie, so I can only assume you're feeling more chipper. Still, you need to rest—we can talk all this over tomorrow."

"I'm a bit tired, but I really don't need to be in a *hospital!* Where is everyone, anyway? Where's the doctor, where are the nurses?"

"The nurse has gone for a break. The doctor will see you on her rounds tomorrow morning. I insisted you stay here the night, just to make sure your B-12 and iron levels return to normal. Well, not *your* normal, as they were far too low, but a *normal* person's normal."

The door flew open. "Hey, I figured I'd get ten minutes before they chucked me out. Man, it's dark in here. Where are your gatekeepers?" It was Star bursting into the room with a huge box of chocolates and a basket of fruit. "No point bringing flowers if you'll only be here a night. That's what they told me on the phone. Hi, Daniel, we met a long time ago at the Vanity Fair Oscar party."

He stood up. "That's right. You won that year for best actress for *Skye's The Limit.*" They awkwardly shuffled about, not knowing if they should kiss cheeks or shake hands, although Star's arms were full, so the two of them kind of blew kisses in the air. The type of greeting I knew Daniel hated with a vengeance. Well, Star blew kisses, he sort of half winced, half smiled.

"Well, I'll be off then," he said. "Nice seeing you, Star." He bent down and let his head rest beside mine and breathed me in, inhaling my hair. I was glad I'd washed it that day or I would have felt awkward. He stayed that way for several beats as if he just didn't want to leave me but felt forced to because of Star's presence. His lips rested on my cheek without actually kissing me. Then he finally whispered, "Please take more care of yourself, Jamie. I don't know what I'd do if I lost you. See you tomorrow." He squeezed my limp hand and then left the room.

"Only five more minutes," a voice said, peeping through the doorway. It was a whippet-thin nurse wearing horn-rimmed glasses. She looked like she belonged in another era. "You need some light in here."

The room flooded white with hospital glare, and the nurse disappeared. I was still reeling from Daniel's apparent one hundred and eighty degree turn. Desperately concerned. Personally involved. Invested in me. As if I were his bona fide girlfriend.

"I had a heart attack when they told me you were here, even though I heard it wasn't life threatening," Star said, ripping open the chocolate box.

"Who let you know?"

"Pearl."

"This whole thing's pretty crazy. I had no idea at all that I was anemic. I mean, years ago I suspected, and I had myself checked over, but they told me I was fine."

"That was a surprise, seeing Daniel here." Star popped a chocolate into my mouth and then chose one for herself.

"He was here when I woke up," I said, the toffee in the chocolate sticking between my teeth. "Am I allowed to eat these? I mean, it doesn't mess with my sugar levels or something, does it?"

"The more you eat right now, the better. You're not diabetic, you're just anemic."

"Anyway, he was staring at me, watching me sleep. If I wasn't so crazy about him I would have been creeped out."

"Yeah, well, he is kind of giving you mixed messages."

I nodded. Star was right. "The latest message is that he's going to play opposite me in the movie, as well as directing—he's back in the picture, in more ways than one. Simon got fired. Cal got fired. Damn it, I forgot to ask Daniel about Cal! I'll call Cal later. Crap! All this has been so crazy and intense!"

Star stopped chewing. "What? Daniel wants to direct the movie again? And play the leading role? I thought he didn't want anything to do with

Samuel Myers!"

"Samuel Myers has given him artistic and crea-tive control and is going to let Daniel do whatever he wants now."

"Which is?"

"Shoot the sex scenes in black and white and make it all arty and classy. Or so he says."

Star grabbed a bunch of grapes. "I can see why you're all riled up about him. There's no denying that he's very hot. Jeez, did you see his eyes?"

"I know," I said helplessly. *Those eyes* that had been my undoing for all these years. *Those eyes* that ripped through the very fabric of my being. "You think I haven't noticed?"

Star shoved five grapes into her mouth at once. "So you'll do the movie, right? I mean you have to."

I told her the whole story, about how the no-nudity clause would be null and void and how I'd be Daniel's pawn, putting my trust in him com-pletely if I said yes.

She moved onto an apple. Something told me the fruit hamper and chocolates were her break-fast, lunch, and dinner. "Stop being so fussy. Just do the goddamn movie already and enjoy yourself."

"This is a far cry from your earlier advice, Star, when you warned me to keep away from him because he was fucking Natasha Jürgen looka-likes."

"This is work. He's got great artistic taste and is very respected as a director. The movie will be well received and look great. Just be professional about it. Think of it as a job—which it is."

I remembered what Daniel said about Star—that she was a veteran, born into this world. Strong. Not fazed by anything. Wished I could be more like her. "So how does it work, exactly, on set, when you do heavy sex scenes?" I asked.

"Well, the set will be closed. That includes everybody except the director, cameraperson, sound, and wardrobe."

"Wardrobe? But I'll be naked except for my privacy patch and nipple pasties!"

"You'll have your own personal costumer, who'll be there with a robe to cover you the second you need it, in between takes, don't worry."

I nervously twiddled a lock of hair. "There are BDSM themes in this movie—stuff like that."

"Believe me, it's so technical—as you discovered already—that it's just like any other day of shooting. The only difference is you're almost naked. First day is awkward and then it's a breeze."

"The real reason that's killing me? I'm so obsessed with Daniel and I know working with him every day . . . kissing . . . and these sex scenes and . . . well, I'm going to fall even harder, and I know he's still in love with his late wife and he'll never—"

"Janie, he's really into you, I can tell."

"You think so? I'm so crazy about him, it makes me sick. I mean . . . literally sick. Look at me."

"You can't blame Daniel for your lazy eating habits."

"You noticed, huh?"

"He'll come around eventually, you'll see. The good thing is you'll be able to keep tabs on him because you'll be seeing each other every day. As director *and* leading man? Trust me, he simply won't have time in his schedule for fucking Natasha Jürgen lookalikes."

STAR LEFT, AND THE NURSE gave me a sponge bath, and then my dinner. My period had ebbed away so at least I didn't have to worry about that. I mulled over what Star had said; she was right. I needed to be professional. Think of it as a job and nothing else. I grabbed my phone and scrolled through my messages. Two from Star, one from Pearl, one from my dad saying how excited he was that we'd be seeing each other (when was that arranged?), and one from Will announcing they were coming for a visit. News to me. But I missed them and felt a surge of excitement. Even though New York wasn't far from Vermont, I didn't get to see them that often. I hadn't told them I was in the hospital, and by the sound of both messages, they had no idea I was here. As far as I knew, nobody had their numbers to call them, anyway.

There was a text message from Daniel wishing me a good night's rest. I wondered why Cal hadn't gotten in touch and then reminded myself of how badly he'd been treated. Perhaps he felt betrayed by me in some way. We still hadn't spoken since yesterday. I'd call him—we needed to talk, and up until now, I simply hadn't had a chance.

Cal answered on the third ring.

"Janie," he said, "so sorry I didn't call." *He* was

apologizing? I felt instantly guilty.

"Cal, so great to hear your voice. I'm sorry I haven't called either, but I got taken to the hospital—nothing terrible, don't worry."

"I know," he said.

"Oh, really? Who told you?"

"I was just leaving for the airport when there was a commotion and they called 911 after you fainted. There was nothing I could do; my plane was set to leave."

"Yeah, Daniel told me. He sent you to New York in his private jet."

"Cool, huh?"

"*Cool?* Cal, you were basically fired from the movie, how can that be *cool?*"

"You didn't hear?"

"Hear what?" I asked, confused. Cal sounded like he was about to explode with happiness, I could hear his big grin over the phone, wrapped like a ribbon, around his voice box.

"I got a major TV role. The lead in a pilot that's going to be shot in Vancouver."

I exhaled a gust of relief. "That's incredible! Great timing, what a coincidence!"

"Well, not really, Daniel got me the part."

"He's the director? I don't understand."

"No, silly, how can he be the director when he's already doing *The Dark Edge of Love*? His friend, who's the producer, owed Daniel a big favor, and he cast me with no audition, just from my video clips of work I've done. Isn't that amazing? I mean, *The Dark Edge of Love* was huge but this is five times the money, plus I get to keep my *Dark Edge of Love* fee, plus extra severance on top, courtesy of Pearl's generosity—she didn't have to do that—my agent was amazed. So I'm, like, stinking of fragrant roses right now. If the TV show's a hit, it could run for years. Everyone knows the kudos is with TV now, with shows like *Breaking Bad* and *Game of Thrones* . . . film has lost its power." He was almost breathless with delight. He'd obviously forgotten all about our road trip to Santa Barbara.

He rambled on, "My part is great, too. I play a corrupt cop who also sees visions . . . you know like Christopher Walken in that movie, *The Dead Zone*? Well, it's like that, all mixed up with politics, a bit like *House of Cards* meets *The Dead Zone*, meets whatever that show was called with Patricia Arquette, but my part is kind of like—"

"When were you going to tell me all this?" I cut in, a little hurt. He hadn't even texted me. I was the last to know! And, as for Daniel procuring this part for him, why hadn't Daniel told me himself what he was up to?

"Sorry, Janie, I just felt a little weird, you know? I guess a bit guilty getting special treatment from Daniel. I see what you mean—he's very cool, very generous."

I wanted to enlighten him to the fact that Daniel had ulterior motives, that his "generosity" was laced with selfish intentions, but didn't want to wound Cal's pride. "You know Daniel will be replacing you as my leading man?" I said tentatively. "I mean, he himself is going to act opposite me."

"Yeah, I know, good luck. Hey, Janie, I've gotta go, have to be up at the crack of dawn—a car's coming for me so I need to get some shuteye."

"You're already about to start filming?"

"Have to go shopping with Wardrobe."

The ego of every actor. I'd forgotten that. It seemed all Cal was interested in was himself and his part. He hadn't even asked if I was okay. "Well, have fun, keep me posted. And congratulations,

Cal."

"Thanks, see you around, Janie."

I pressed END and felt a lone tear fall down my cheek. *See you around.* So much for Cal being boyfriend material! Typical actor behavior. Self-centered. I'm-alright-Jack.

My mind wandered back to Daniel. He obviously *did* care about me; his manipulative hiring and firing proved it. I *knew* he felt something for me. But still, I did *not* want to be his rebound relationship. Just because his late wife was dead and gone did not make me number one in his eyes. He'd told me, to my face, I was the last person in the world he wanted a relationship with. His words: *"I'm feeling very angry right now. I'm in no state to have a relationship, **least of all with you**,"* ricocheted in my brain. I wished I could fast-forward time. Be the sophisticated actress I would be five years hence, when Daniel would be mentally free of Natasha Jürgen and all her beauty, glamor and sophistication, and the lost child they would have had together, and be ready for someone like me. No, not someone like me. **Me**.

Me, me, me, *me*!
Calm down, Janie, get a grip.

I decided I needed to come clean. Tell Daniel how I felt. Clear the air. Confront him about his fuckathon. After all, I was about to get up close and personal with him, what if he'd caught a sexually transmitted disease on his rounds? That flimsy cock-sock he'd be wearing and the miniscule thingy to cover my girly bits would hardly protect me from raging genital herpes or Hepatitis C. I'd insist he get tested and *insist* that he keep clear of other women until we'd finished filming. I could even get my lawyer to write it into my contract.

Yes! I'd do the role, but on certain conditions.

I mentally made a list of my limits:

- No sexual relations with anyone else during filming.

- Mandatory testing for STDs and HIV, with rights to see the doctor's report with my own eyes.

- No tormenting me with sexy talk about fucking me or spanking me. (Or had I imagined that)?

- No kissing me off set or whispering sweet nothings in my ear.

- No cameras or videos allowed on set during filming, other than the main cameras.
- Everyone who is connected with the movie to sign a non-disclosure agreement.

As I was embellishing my mental list by the second, polishing any tarnish off the fine details, my phone rang. There was breathing down the line. At first I thought it was the wrong number, then a dirty caller, then Daniel making a sexy call (wishful thinking), and then I realized it was my brother Will.

"Janie, we're on our way."

"Right now? You caught a plane already? Talk about giving me notice. I didn't even know you were planning on a visit!"

"I can do numbers. I can gamble. I can do numbers. Want to go to Vegas. We can meet there."

"*What?* Vegas? What are you saying, Will? No! Just, no!"

"Dad thinks it's a good idea."

My father had always been somewhat irresponsible, my mom the organizer, the fixer, the one who thought for the two of them. But *this?* This was crazy.

"Will, there are so many things you can do with your life, but going to Vegas and gambling is not one of them."

I had visions of Will being beaten up by the mafia for winning too much money in clandestine ways, left to bleed in a gutter somewhere. Worse, shot in the head. It was true he was clever with math—like a sort of computer, but his therapist always told us that nurturing that facet of his brain would hinder, not help him. It would cause the creative, "social" part of the brain to shut off. He needed to make friends and interact, not hide inside a numerical cocoon.

"Where are you now?" I asked.

"At JFK, changing planes."

"*What*? Why didn't Dad let me know about this?"

"I told him I'd spoken to you and that you said it was great, that we could meet there."

"You lied? That's a lie, Will, I did not say it was okay!"

"We're on our way to Vegas, on our way to Vegas, on our way to—"

"Put Dad on the line."

17

"On our way to Vegas . . . " he sang, and then he was gone.

I frantically dialed Dad's cell. It was off. Crap, crap, *crap*! This was all I needed right now.

2

THE NEXT DAY, after I'd been cleared by the doctor and given a pep talk about how I had to eat more iron-rich foods and take my vitamins, Star came to pick me up from the hospital and took me back to her house. As we drove, she told me all the details about how she had once been kidnapped, amazingly by her brother and some loony Russian, and how she'd fallen in love with her assistant director, who was also acting as her bodyguard—they'd been locked up together, downtown LA. How they were finally freed, but Leo—the guy she loved—got shot, and her brother arrested. I'd read the story once, and seen it all over the news on TV, several years earlier, but had no idea the story had been so complex. It made me understand how vulnerable she was; how, as such a major movie star, she was a walking target. Did I want that kind of attention? *The Dark Edge of Love*—if it did well at the box office—could change my life as I knew it.

I told her the whole Will saga, and Star agreed I should go to Vegas, and even offered to come with me.

"It's fine," I told her. "Really, I can handle it, and I'm okay—I feel rested and strong enough to fly."

She looked doubtful. "*Really?*"

"Really. I'd rather deal with my family alone. No offense, but you know how it is."

"Yeah, I do. Family can be really fucked up."

When I got back to Star's house, I spoke to Dad, who was horrified that Will had fibbed to me, saying what a great idea it was to go to Vegas.

Unfortunately, it was too late to turn the clock back now. Or rather, the *invisible* clock, because we all know that in Vegas they have no clocks. Will had been missing since five a.m., from the hotel. I knew what he was up to: playing in a casino somewhere.

"There's no point in you even coming," Dad

objected. "You're weak and need all your strength—you can't be running around Vegas looking for Will in your condition."

"I'm worried about him, Dad. He could get into serious trouble if they get wind of his game, his method, whatever . . . that is, if he has one."

"He'll be okay," Dad said, sounding unconvinced.

"How much money did he have on him when he left the hotel this morning?" I asked.

"Like fifty dollars, if that."

"Have you searched the hotel?"

"There are four thousand and four rooms here, a casino the size of three football fields, and sixteen restaurants—where should I begin?"

"Well you could start by calling him on his cell, have you tried that?" It seemed like a really obvious thing to say, but my father often bypassed the obvious. Practical was not a word in Dad's personal dictionary.

"He's switched off his cell," he said, his tone hopeless . . . helpless.

"Well I'm coming out."

This time, he didn't protest.

Just as I was stuffing the last things I needed

into an overnight case, my cell buzzed again. Daniel. Normally, I would have lost all concentration with what I was doing and morphed into a panting Daniel Glass groupie, but right now I had no time for him, or his movie.

"I'm running really late, Daniel," I snipped, sitting on my suitcase and zipping it up. "I'll call you later."

"Wait! Janie?"

I hung up. It was rude, but I could *not* be distracted by Daniel Glass, right this minute, not with Will roaming around casinos, with no clocks on the walls. If he'd been missing since five a.m. that meant he'd won money, which meant he'd play until his luck ran out. Where had he even learned to play cards or roulette in the first place? Online? It didn't bear thinking about. He didn't own a credit card; if he had, he probably would have totaled up a grand debt by now. Hence his fascination with Vegas. How dumb could my dad be?

Very dumb, as it happened. You would have never known he had letters to his name and was a bona fide professor. Okay, he was a professor of *music,* so perhaps that did lend a clue as to how on the ball he could be in the real world. But still.

Jake and Star offered to drive me to the airport, but I knew how busy they were, so I convinced them to let me drive myself, since Star had so generously given me *carte blanche* with her car. Apart from a bruise on my right arm where the IV had been, I felt fine. I raced out the door and went flying headfirst into . . .

Daniel.

"What the heck?"

"Janie, I was outside the door when I called you."

"How did you even know where I was?" *Was he stalking me?*

"Good guess. Where are you going?"

I told him the whole saga as I rushed toward the car. He grabbed my case from me and simultaneously pulled me into an embrace. Or *was* it an embrace?

"You're not driving," he ordered.

"Just try and stop me," I foolishly protested, trapped close against his hard chest.

"I *am* stopping you."

"Let me go, Daniel, I have to catch my plane!"

"I'm coming with you, or rather, you're coming with *me*." He entwined his arm around my waist as I shuffled along beside him, trying as I was, to break free. "Don't be silly, Janie, we'll go to Vegas together and we'll take my jet."

"What is it with you and your private jets lately?"

"You are *not* getting on a commercial plane on your own when you've just come out of the hospital. Someone will start sneezing all over you." Just like Daniel. A veritable Howard Hughes when it came to hygiene. "You're coming with me, and I won't hear one more word to the contrary."

He bundled me into his black Mercedes and drove off, both of us traveling in silence, the atmosphere a wall between us. Boy, he annoyed me. Who did he think he was, calling the shots? I didn't have the strength to argue, though, so I slumped into my car seat and gazed out of the window.

It seemed like we arrived seconds later because, apparently, I had dozed off for the entire car ride.

"You see? You were tired," he remarked, as we pulled up to the airport.

I opened one eye and saw a vision of beauty before me. All in black, his hair flopping over one side off his face, a blue eye—turquoise even, speckled with flecks of black—was sizing me up with approval. He parked the car, his wrist casual on the steering wheel, sporting a beautiful, Patek Phillipe watch. Even when Daniel was dressed down, he looked elegant. Never sneakers, but hand-made, Italian, leather shoes. Daniel Glass had my heart pounding again. Was I really about to take a private jet with him to Las Vegas?

"Where are your brother and father staying?" he asked.

"At the Aria. Why?"

"Just wondered if they were at one of mine."

"One of your what?"

"One of my hotels."

"You own hotels now, *too*?"

His mouth lifted into an easy smile. "Part of my inheritance. My father had fingers in many pies."

"And those pies are all yours?"

"Yes."

"You must have very sticky fingers."

He gazed at me for a long beat and said, "I like having sticky fingers."

I realized the innuendo of what he just said. In

my dreams those fingers had been in me and all over me, but in reality all we'd done was kiss. Then I remembered; it wasn't *me* he was referring to but all his blondes. *Ugh!*

"Yes, I've heard all about your roaming hands," I said, trying to sound nonchalant.

He got out of the car and closed the door with a loud clunk. What I said obviously irked him. *Yes, the truth can hurt.* I mentally geared myself up to confront him about this pertinent issue and let him know in no uncertain terms what I would and would not accept if I were to take the part of Sylvie. I still hadn't said yes to doing the movie.

He came around to my side and opened the door for me. "Let's go," he said in his low, no-nonsense voice. "We can talk on the plane—we patently need to clear a few things up." *Patently.* I smiled. His choice of vocabulary was always succinct—he used words that were so out of style they almost sounded hip.

The jet was outrageous. I could see why Cal had been so impressed. Smooth leather seats, and conference tables, plush carpeting. All this was Daniel's private property? I realized that for all my Wikipedia and Google stalking, and hours, weeks, and months in rehearsal with Daniel, I actually knew very little about him.

"I know nothing about you, really," I pointed out, lying back in my seat after I'd buckled up. We were about to take off.

"Your imagination, Janie, runs away with you. You assume things about me that simply aren't true."

"My imagination? Am I imagining this swanky jet and the fact that you are basically a billionaire?"

He swiped his hand through the air, waving away my observation. "It's company money, I don't consider it mine."

"Oh, so you have a bunch of shareholders?"

"No, I own the company outright."

"So let me get this straight; you own the company outright yet you don't consider it yours?"

"Of course it's mine."

"Yet the money isn't? That doesn't make sense."

He laughed, his wide smile spreading across his face. He looked amazing when he laughed—so carefree. "You're right, what I said was preposterous."

He put his hand on my thigh—tingles shot

down to my toes and up to my dizzy head. He edged closer to me, even though the plane was steaming along the runway, about to lift off. "Look," he said, "I think you've got the wrong impression. What you said in the car unnerved me. About roaming hands. What was that supposed to mean?"

"The word is that you have quite a reputation, Daniel Glass. And to be honest with you, I'm not interested in shooting this movie with someone who could be riddled with sexually transmitted diseases." *There, I said it.*

He burst out laughing again.

"I'm serious, Daniel. What you do is your business, but if I'm to be pretty much naked, with you all over me, I want to know you're as clean as a whistle."

He tried to put on a serious face. "I haven't had sex with anyone since my wife died," he said, still chuckling to himself.

"Yeah, right."

"Janie, I don't know what gossip you've heard, but I can assure you, I've been far too busy to run around looking for pu . . . possibilities of hook-ups."

"That's not what half of Hollywood says. Seems like you have a penchant for busty blondes."

He stared at me. Hard. "Actually, if you really want to know, I have a 'penchant'—as you say—for petite, undernourished brunettes."

His half-lie made my stomach flip. "Okay, then you won't mind getting tested."

"No, not at all. If it makes you happy, then fine. You can get tested too."

"What, *me?*"

"Yes, you. I don't know where Cal's been, or anyone else you might have had relations with."

"I . . . nothing happened with Cal!"

"That's not what I heard."

"What? Who from? Him? We had a little itty bitty kiss, nothing more."

"Tell that to half of Hollywood."

"It's gossip!"

"Well, there you go, gossip has a way of traveling its way into people's gullible ears and straight out the other side, without even a thought as to whom it could be hurting."

I puffed in protestation. "Well, I don't fuck around, just so you know."

"And nor do I, just so you know," he said in an even voice.

I glared at him. I supposed it was *possible* that this was all gossip. Yet he was so sexy and handsome, and ridiculously successful, not to mention loaded, and I knew women were throwing themselves at him any chance they got. I eyed him warily.

"Anyway, you're still in love with your wife," I added, like a petulant child asking for someone else's share of candy.

"What do you mean by that, Janie?"

"I mean what I say, that you're in love with her."

"And if that were to be true, why should it affect you?"

"It would make it complicated for the film."

"Ah, I see. So my being 'in love' with my wife would affect your decision about whether to take the role of Sylvie or not?"

His words cut me. The way he laid it out so . . . so . . . blatantly made me look like an ingénue idiot. He had a point. I was a professional actress and I was being absurd. I could feel my lips pouting—I had no answer to his question.

"Are you jealous?" he asked.

My fake laugh would have fooled any audience, and I hoped Daniel too. "How can I possibly be jealous?"

"You're answering my question with a question." He lowered his voice and said in a sensual whisper, "Are you jealous, Janie? Does the idea of my loving someone else torment you?" He brushed my lip with his thumb.

I felt a lump gather in my throat and my eyes flood until they burned. Hot tears slid down my cheek. Talk about wearing your heart on your sleeve. And my heart was like fragile glass.

"I thought so." He smirked a little. What a bastard! He was getting off on this! Having me so desperately into him while he still held a flame for Natasha freaking Jürgen!

I turned my face away from him so he couldn't humiliate me any further, but he held me by the jaw and forced me to look at him, unbuckling his seatbelt, getting down on his knees so he was kneeling in front of me. The fact that the plane hadn't stabilized didn't deter him.

"Look into my eyes," he demanded. "Look at me, Janie, and tell me how you really feel."

I was blubbering now. The pathetic little student in love with her teacher, the lapdog who would follow her master off a cliff. *Why can't I be stronger than that?*

"Are you in love with me, Janie?" He unbuckled my seatbelt and, at the same time his hand brushed across my belly, his fingers feeling for my flesh, his touch light. I let him continue, too weak to protest, too stunned by his cruelty at causing me to fall apart. "Are you in love with me, Janie," his echo murmured into my mouth—not even saying it as a question, but as a statement—his hand reaching inside my jeans and slipping down under the thin fabric of my panties. I gasped. His tongue found my mouth, prying my lips apart.

"No," I whimpered into his mouth, "I'm not."

He hooked his other hand around the waistband of my jeans and started pulling them down.

"Oh, fuck," he said, his fingers gliding inside me. I was soaked. This was real, not a dream, and it was different from any of my fantasies. Even more intense.

My eyelids fluttered in submission as his thumb found my clit and pressed on it like a button, all the while his fingers sliding in and out of me.

"Because I could swear that you were completely crazy about me," he said, taking my lip between his teeth. I moaned. His free hand trailed up my stomach and circled my nipples, one by one, not touching them. I found myself bucking my hips at him, eager for the extra contact with his thumb on my hard nub. "But then again . . . you've put up quite a fight," he murmured.

My jeans and panties were somehow halfway down my thighs now, and I vaguely wondered where the airplane steward was; if he'd find me in this semi-naked state. Daniel's lips trailed from my lips to my breasts, which he started licking one by one, and then sucking each nipple individually. Hard.

"Oh, God," I groaned. My seat had been pushed back in my delirium, and my pants were even lower. Daniel's mouth traveled south, and in one aggressive tug he yanked my panties down all the way and pressed his head between my thighs. His tongue took over from his thumb and fingers, as he growled into my pussy, eating, nipping, sucking me into his mouth. It felt amazing.

"Please," I cried out.

He carried on, flicking his tongue at my clit now, lashing it with lightning fast strokes to the point of torture. It was too much—the sensation too much.

"Fuck me, Daniel . . . please."

He knelt up, looked into my eyes, then stood up. I could see the hard ridge—that bulge I'd seen before, massive and intimidating. He bent down and scooped me up in his arms and carried me to a private cabin, where he plunked me on a bed. I watched him as he took a condom out of his pocket, and ripped the foil packet with his teeth.

This was it; Daniel Glass was going to fuck me. Finally.

For real this time.

He started to unbuckle his belt, then unbuttoned his black trousers, as I stared transfixed at the apparition before my greedy eyes. He came closer, his crotch level with my face.

"Is this what you want, Janie?"

I nodded.

"It's all yours."

I sat up and brought my trembling hands up to his hips. I slowly unfastened his fly as his cock flexed beneath the fabric of his pants. I laid my hand on his mountain and sucked in a sharp breath. It was rock hard and even bigger to my touch than I expected. "You're huge," I said. He was. *Huge.*

He clenched his eyes shut and parted his beautiful mouth as my fingers nervously grappled with the stubborn fabric. I hadn't done this up until now, and I was shaking. I'd had one serious boyfriend in my life and he had never asked me to undress him. Finally, the pants slid off Daniel's hips. My gaze fixed on his boxer briefs—my next hurdle. The bulge was even more enormous—the outline of his throbbing crown reaching up to his navel in a thick solid arrow—and I shuddered, wondering how it could possibly fit inside me. I hadn't had sex for so long, I could hardly even remember how it all worked. Would this be painful? My ex didn't have this kind of equipment— then again, I had never felt so ready for anyone in my life as I did now.

I touched his ridge with my lips, then nibbled him there, my teeth sinking tentatively into the combed cotton of Daniel's boxer briefs.

"Fuck, Janie," he groaned, opening his eyes and casting his gaze down at me. I continued to nip along the long, thick shaft, too scared to take off his underwear and reveal his mammoth erection in the flesh. He made my mind up for me, by pulling off his boxer briefs so his cock sprang free. He grasped it in both hands. "I'd fucking love it if you took me in your sexy mouth. Open up."

I did as I was told, and he eased himself into my mouth, a deep guttural groan emanating from his throat as he did so. I felt a rush of moisture shoot between my thighs, and my clit started to pound with longing. I had never felt such an ache or yearning before, and I feared it—I could sense myself losing control. He started languidly fucking my mouth, his hands clawing my hair as he guided my lips up and down his massive length.

"I want thizz inthide of may," I gagged.

He stopped mid-plunge and said, "You're sure?"

"Oh, yeah."

He slowly pulled out. "Fuck, you're sexy, Janie, "you make me fucking ravenous for you. You're sure?" he asked again. I nodded. "Because I could hurt you without meaning to."

What he said unnerved me, but I licked my lips, which he took as a cue to condom-up. He rolled the thing on and I wished we didn't have to use it. It spoiled the aesthetic nature of the scene—no wonder you never saw them in the movies. Still, I had to be careful, just in case his blonde bimbo denial was a bald-faced lie.

He went down on his knees again and yanked me toward him, edging open my thighs so I was splayed out wide. He prized them even further apart. Lying on top of me, he rested the crest of his massive dick at my entrance, tickling me teasingly, gently prodding me but not entering.

"Please, Daniel."

"Please what?"

"I need you inside me."

"How much? How much do you need me, Janie?"

I moaned and writhed about, bucking my pelvis as close as I could get so his cock pulsed inside me a touch. But he drew back, his willpower strong. He wasn't about to enter me in a hurry. "Tell me you need me."

I didn't say a word, just grabbed his ass and thrashed my hips up at him. He was on an ego trip. Wanted to hear how desperate I was for him, and I didn't want to admit it, although once he started rubbing his thick erection against my clit, massaging his huge cock up and down, I was squirming for more.

"Please fuck me, Daniel. Pleeease."

He kept up his torture until I was on the edge, desperate to come. He kissed me—a deep, long kiss that spoke of sex and lust, and dare I say it? . . . love. And then the actual words that I'd been fantasizing about for years spilled from his lips right into my mouth:

"I love you, Janie. I do."

Why couldn't I believe him? I wanted to . . . but feared what he said was in the heat of the moment, a moment which I needed to accept for what it was . . . hot sex.

"Tell me you love me," he goaded. His ego-trip again. What he'd told me about not being ready for a relationship flashed through my brain. But I craved this; to be able to disassociate the sex from my psychological need for him.

I shook my head in the negative—I knew getting love and sex mixed into one lethal cocktail was a big mistake. "Just fuck me," I answered, my tone unintentionally cold.

"You really want to fuck, Janie, is that it?"

Then his raspy voice softened and he added, "You want to *fuck* or you want me to make love to you?"

"I want you to fuck me really hard," I whispered into his mouth, this beautiful mouth that was on me now—lips on mine, tongue inside me, eating me alive.

He plunged himself inside me on the word "fuck" and started pounding hard, filling me up with his size, groaning with each stroke. This was hot.

I hooked my legs around his thighs and my arms around his torso to give myself leverage. He was fucking me like I was a whore, grinding into me ruthlessly, groaning about how hot and tight and wet I was. I suddenly couldn't handle it. Not one bit. I wanted to be his plaything but there was no way I could go along with it.

"Please stop!" I cried. Tears were streaming down my face.

He did. Immediately. Then he pulled out, which was even worse. I felt bereft and lonely and started sobbing hopelessly. But he gathered me into a hug, so close against his chest I felt the steady rhythm of his heart.

"So stubborn, Janie. So, *so* stubborn, it's a

joke!" He kissed the tip of my nose and my forehead, and squeezed my sobbing little body tight, cocooning me inside his muscular arms. "We don't have to play this silly game, you know," he said, "we can talk all this through."

I cried a good deal more, feeling like a fool to think I could handle Daniel Glass and his huge great cock without getting emotionally involved. Of course I couldn't just fuck him. Impossible. I wanted his soul. Which was also impossible. I was screwed up in the head. And way too needy. The situation was useless.

"I love you, Janie," he said unexpectedly.

I looked up at him in disbelief. He was trying to make me feel better, which was sweet of him, but "love" was a strong word and one I was sure he wasn't truly ready for.

"You're convinced I'm still in love with Natasha Jürgen, aren't you?" Weird . . . to call his wife by her full name.

"It's normal," I said. "It's only been—"

He cut me short, "We were going to get divorced, you know." He carefully wiped away my tears with his thumb.

I looked at him, bleary eyed. "But you were

crazy about each other."

"That's what the papers say, but in reality? Our marriage was a sham."

"*What?*"

"She betrayed me, Janie. She had a lover." He punched out the word lover.

Impossible! Who, in their right mind, would chose another man over Daniel! No, no! He had it wrong; his own paranoia—jealousy perhaps—for being married to such a blonde bombshell.

"I doubt it," I said, a wry, knowing smile playing on my lips. *Impossible.*

"Janie, I'm not making this up, it's a fact."

I breathed in his scent: sex, soap, a musky Daniel Glass smell that was unique to him. "Who? *Why?* Why did she have a lover when she had *you?*"

"I couldn't offer her what she needed—or wanted."

"But the baby!" I gasped, "Natasha was pregnant."

His eyes flashed sharp—a flinty, gleaming pain. "How do you know about that?"

I was about to say 'Wikipedia' but realized how stalkerish that sounded. "Rumor, I guess."

"Well rumor was right. She was pregnant with

another man's baby."

"I'm sorry." But I wasn't sorry, I was secretly gleeful. Maybe now I could lay to rest the ghost of the perfect, stainless, impeccable Natasha Jürgen. I still couldn't believe he had his facts right, though. "How do you know it wasn't yours?"

"They did a paternity test, a DNA test on the dead fetus, at my request."

"I'm sorry," I said again, meaning it this time. The word 'dead' hit it home to me. A poor innocent baby: dead.

We lay there together, our pants around our respective ankles after our disastrous coupling, listening to each other's heartbeats and finding solace in a new-found friendship based on trust. I wasn't the only one who had a heart made of glass. The idea that Daniel could be damaged, vulnerable, and wounded by someone, had not ever occurred to me. That's why he wanted to know if I was in love with him. Not to feed his ego, but to ensure himself that my feelings were genuine. I saw him in a whole new light.

He continued to open himself up to me, revealing his past, his hurt and grief—never for a moment feeling sorry for himself, though, but more like clarifying why he hadn't felt ready for another relationship. Natasha dying had made things even more complicated, he explained. Emotions bubbled over, he said: guilt, anger, sadness, a sense of failure. He told me how Natasha had wanted a glamorous lifestyle and he'd deduced—after she took up with a billionaire, Argentinean polo-player—how she must have married Daniel primarily for his money, but then felt let down when he didn't provide the swanky lifestyle to go with it.

"Not my style," he said.

And I, being so in love with him, found this inconceivable, but I also found it inconceivable that men had cheated on Marilyn Monroe. The human heart is hard to fathom; people's behavior can be bizarre.

Everything made sense to me now. The reason for Daniel pulling back, diving into the pool, that time, to cool himself down after our kiss. He wanted me, but didn't trust himself not to hurt me. The film had acted as a catalyst to pull us together, something he hadn't been entirely ready for. He had been left a broken man. Maybe too broken to fix. I didn't want to be his rebound.

"Do you still feel angry with Natasha?" I asked. Wounds like these left scars.

"It is what it is," Daniel said, not giving anything away. He got up and put his clothes back on. I watched his every movement, gauging his mood, second-guessing his thoughts.

My doubts crept back, nestling in my gut like an incurable virus. I pulled up my panties and then my jeans. I felt less vulnerable dressed. "Were you crazy about her?" I asked warily, not wanting to hear the answer, yet not being able to tear myself away from this insidiously fascinating subject: Natasha Jürgen.

"I guess I was dazzled by her, but the truth is we were incompatible from the word go."

"Is that why she went looking elsewhere?"

"No. Her relationship with Ricardo had started before we were even married."

I felt a stab to my chest on Daniel's behalf. "*What?* That's insane! What was she *thinking?*" Heat rushed to my ears. Fury at her cruelty.

"She wanted to have her cake and eat it too. Ricardo was married—you know what those Latin American Catholics can be like—and his wife wouldn't give him a divorce. Natasha was his lover and he took her all over the world—private jets, super yachts, helicopters, Gstaad and Mustique in winter, Patagonia in summer. His wife momentarily grabbed his attention back by getting pregnant. That's when Natasha married me. She swore it was over between them, but it wasn't. Her goal was to win him back, give him a son so she could recapture his heart, once and for all."

"She sounds like a real number," I said, "using you that way. And the baby? Could they tell what it was? *Was* she going to have a boy?"

"It was a girl, apparently. Lost her poor little life at the same time as Natasha—no oxygen to the brain, nothing could be done to save either of them."

The way he said it sounded as if he missed Natasha horribly. "Did you love her?" I asked outright. Again, the seed of jealously replanting itself. Ready to sprout.

"I loved the person I thought I knew. But it's hard being in love with a lie."

My heart beat fast as I prepared my next question. I had to know. "So where does that leave us?"

He pulled me into a tighter embrace. "It leaves

us free from lies," he told me. "Free to really get to know each other, to learn to trust one another, and to work together professionally without fear. Do you trust me, Janie?"

My pulse pounded, more blood rushing to my head. Total trust? That was a tall order. I decided to be honest. "I've spent all this time being so in love with you, Daniel, and terrified about you hurting me, so trust is something you'll have to earn from me. Does that make sense?"

He cocked a small, resigned smile. "It makes perfect sense."

"Could you be faithful to me?" I quizzed, my eyes searching for the truth in his answer.

"I'd never do to you what Natasha did to me, so yes, I can be faithful. I'm not the cheating kind, anyway."

"You swear, then, that it's just gossip about you screwing all those Natasha Jürgen lookalikes?"

He roared with laughter, the skin at the edge of his blue eyes creasing with mirth. "Natasha Jürgen lookalikes? I can assure you the real thing was bad enough, I won't be seeking more of the same. Who started that crazy rumor?"

I didn't want to put Star and Jake in the middle

of it, so I didn't let on. I thought of Cindy Spektor, whom I had also silently accused. "That's what people say, that all the women were blond, busty, Natasha Jürgen lookalikes."

He was still smiling. "Just for the record, she wasn't that busty in reality. She had a lot of help in the wardrobe department."

"Oh."

"I know what you're thinking, Janie, and, no, I'm not into huge breasts. I happen to love yours just the way they are, so don't get it into your head to go all Hollywood on me and change yourself."

Although his compliment bolstered me up, my head was still immersed in Natasha like a submarine submerged in water, refusing to come up for air. "She may have been far more beautiful than me, but I can top her in the loyalty stakes."

He took both my hands in his and kissed them. "Janie, why, why, why, have you no idea how ravishing you are? Isn't it completely obvious when you look in the mirror each day?"

I shook my head, my lack of self-confidence showing through the cracks of insecurity. I thought of how I'd broken down in tears just ten minutes before while having sex—I was as good as a novice. I wouldn't even be able to say I now belonged to the Mile High Club. "It's all about big round butts these days and curves and I'm just a—"

"You're a true beauty, my precious Janie. Did Audrey Hepburn have a big round ass and huge great tits?"

An amused smile at the thought of my icon, Audrey, with a sexy big butt, lifted the corners of my mouth. "No."

"Well, then."

A knock at our cabin door took us by surprise. "We're getting ready for landing, Sir, Ma'am, please buckle up."

"Thank you," Daniel called out. "Janie, we'll continue this conversation at the hotel, after you've found your brother."

"By the way, my brother's . . . different," I wavered, not finding the right adjective for Will.

"Like how?"

"You'll see. He's kind of unpredictable. Whatever he says or does, though, please go easy on him."

"Alright."

"Promise?"

"I promise."

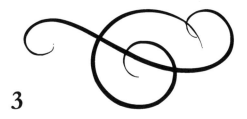

3

I HAD ONLY BEEN to Vegas once before, when I was really little. My parents took me to a *Grateful Dead* concert; a reunion of the band, at the height of summer, sometime in August. If you could imagine the hottest day you'd experienced in your life and then put a hairdryer to your face, that's how stifling it was. They were giving out Gatorade for free, which impressed me, and everyone was going around with plant sprayers full of water, to spray on their bodies and faces. There was a hose on, full-time, to cool people down. It was all happening in the open air during the day. I guessed it went on until the evening, too, but I was in bed by that point. The main thing I remember is people laughing their heads off. All day long. Wild, jaw-aching laughing, giant smiles splitting their faces in two. Years later, I realized that people were high on ecstasy or acid, or whatever. My mom admitted to me that Dad had taken magic mushrooms.

Daniel dropped me off at my hotel and left to go to his own. He had told me he owned a string of them, but one in particular he favored, as close as you could get to a "boutique" hotel in this crazy town. I was relieved—I didn't feel comfortable enough to share my family with him. Not yet, anyway.

It wasn't roasting hot here in Vegas, now, and dad wasn't running around grinning and high on hallucinogenics, but I was still dealing with a man who was less than responsible. I spotted him from afar, wandering around the huge swimming pool, cellphone in hand, a forlorn little-boy-lost look on his handsome, chiseled face. My dad had the look of a 1950's movie star—vintage handsome.

My father's lustrous brown eyes searched the surrounding area keenly, as if Will would be by the pool, picking up chicks in bikinis, instead of out on a mission to test his skills as a gambler. So far, Will had shown no interest whatsoever in girls. It was as if he'd been mentally arrested at the age of eleven, although physically everything was more than normal. In fact, Will was downright gorgeous to look at. It had gotten us into some interesting situations in the past; girls trying to hit on him, clueless as he was. Once he'd invited a very pretty nineteen-year-old to "stay over." His idea of staying over was full pajamas, a midnight snack, and a horror movie. When she tried to kiss him he'd said "gross", wrinkling his nose and wiping her kiss off his face.

"Dad," I called out, racing up to my father and encircling him in a bear hug. "I've missed you!"

"Honey, thank God you're here. I've been worried sick about Will wandering around Vegas, losing money in some . . . some crazy gambling hall." It was now five o'clock, he'd been missing for twelve hours. Dad's restless eyes flickered over my shoulder. A waiter walked by with a tray full of drinks.

"Have you called the police?" I asked.

"Yeah, but they pretty much laughed. A twenty-one-year-old guy loose in Vegas? They have bigger issues to deal with, like murder and rape."

"Did you explain?"

"I reported him missing and they filed the details into their computerized local system—fat lot of good it'll do—they made it clear that being a voluntary missing person is *not a crime* and any adult person can simply walk away from his or her family."

"Yes, but, Will isn't—"

"They told me because it's not a crime, the law enforcement is limited on how they handle these type of investigations. If it were a result of a criminal act, they said, they'd take it more seriously. I told them it was endangerment to Will himself, and *maybe to others*, and that's what got their attention, when they finally put him in their database." Dad's words rushed out in a breathy torrent. Will had been living peacefully at home, and in a twenty-mile radius, not venturing anywhere risky except for the fantasylands of his video games. This phenomenon of Will going MIA was new to us both.

"I'm sure he'll turn up soon." As I said this, my eyes focused on a scene in the distance at the far end of the pool, near a cluster of palm trees. A guy was lying face down on a sun lounger, surrounded by three bikini-clad blondes, apparently fawning over his every movement. I knew that body. Or did I? I shook the idea out of my head. The man was being massaged with sun cream; deft fingers traveled seductively down the backs of his firm legs.

"What is it?" Dad said.

"Dad, I'm going to the other end of the pool area to check something out, won't be a minute. Meet you by the bar?"

"Sure," he agreed. "I could use some water."

"Get me a Coke, I'll be right back."

I wandered over, in my flip flops, wondering if the vision I was seeing was my overactive imagination playing tricks on me. The way you do when you have something at the forefront of your mind . . . you see things when they aren't really there. Because, unless someone had spiked my food earlier, I was seeing triple. I rubbed my eyes to make sure.

I stood there, silently, feeling like a fool, as if everything I had been flipping over in my mind about this person in the last twenty-four hours was completely false.

The woman who was massaging his legs was no more than nineteen. Purring over him like a kitten with a bowlful of cream. Another was feeding him a cocktail—a Tequila Sunrise maybe, because the red and gold of the drink swirled about the glass in colorful waves, as he sipped through a long straw. She fingered his dark hair— her scarlet nails keen as little knives; a lock was hanging over his brow.

"Loving this, girls . . . loving it," he murmured, while the third—one with a very sexy round behind—began to massage his nut-brown back.

The younger girl looked up at me, her heavy blond mane hanging over one eye. "Can I help you?" she asked suspiciously, even possessively— there was no room for a petite brunette in their ménage quartet. I wasn't sure, could she? Should I say something?

But I didn't speak, as I knew he'd recognize my voice, so I just shook my head. Then walked away.

Dumbstruck, I ambled back to Dad and sat with him by the bar.

He handed me my drink. "Honey, what's up?"

"Will," I said, "will be just fine."

Dad glugged down a whole glass of water and let out a satisfied gasp. "I wish I could believe that."

"Trust me, dad, he's fine."

"How do you know?"

"Let's just say I have evidence."

"You *saw* him?"

"Yeah," I said, in a dazed monotone, "I saw him."

"And? Where the fuck *is* he?" My parents were never the kind to stop swearing in front of the children—my dad was like a friend, not a typical father.

"He's occupied with a bunch of . . . " –I wanted to say 'girls' but they were too worldly for that—"females," I spluttered. "I didn't want to break the spell for him—the older sister clucking around like a mother hen, you know."

"Whores?"

"Ssh, keep your voice down. I don't think so . . . just opportunists. I don't want to disturb him. He's 'scored,' you know, and this could be his first time—I mean this *must* be his first, surely? I don't want to ruin his Vegas experience."

I assumed Will had won money, but then again, he was damn good looking. Even so . . . *three?*

I expected my father to feel proud of his son initiating his manhood, but he brought up a very good point: "You think he knows about safe sex, Janie? I doubt it. And what if they're all taking copious amounts of drugs?"

"Good point," I said, feeling like the child now. I couldn't believe my dad was so on the ball, for once. "You're right."

He glared at me. "So, where is he?"

"At the other end of the pool. He didn't look like he was going anywhere fast, though. I'll try calling again." I took my cell out from my shorts' pocket. Will's phone jumped to voicemail, just as I expected. I didn't bother leaving a message, I'd already left so many already. "Okay, Dad, I'll go over and . . ." –I didn't know what my plan was, but Dad was agitated, and I thought it best I spoke to Will alone—"you stay here."

I walked over to Will and his harem of girls, mulling over how stunned Dad and I were by Will's new independence manifesting in a way neither of us had ever anticipated. My brother was sitting up now, and our gazes instantly met. A slow smile crept on his face—a face which looked older than I remembered, and less boyish. I hadn't seen him in more than six months.

"Hey," I said, leaning down to kiss him on the cheek. "See you've set yourself up nicely. Dad and I've been calling you non stop."

He squinted at me, the sun in his eyes. "You didn't get my message?"

"Noooo, Will, we've been checking our cells every five minutes!" I tried to stay calm.

"Candy, Stacey, Jill, this is my sister, Janie."

"Hi," I said, trying not to be unfriendly. It wasn't their fault.

Will spoke with a grin, like a giant sticker, slapped across his handsome face. My glare did not deter his happiness for one second. "I left a message early this morning with the concierge, there should be a note . . . a note . . . in Dad's inbox," he said, beaming.

"What happened to your cellphone?"

"I dove in the pool with it by mistake. I have it, but it's not so happy, not so happy. I won a lot of money, Janie, at Blackjack. Won a lot of money."

The last thing Will needed was to be boasting in public about all the money he'd made.

"Will, can I just . . . Dad's worried sick . . . can

we just talk in private for a second?"

He lifted his hands in a gesture, as if to say, *See how annoying my sister is?* "Sure," he said. He reluctantly moved away from scarlet fingernailed Jill, whose talons were still gently rested on his bronzed shoulders, and stood up. He'd grown since I last saw him. He was now well over six feet tall. He'd been working out, too. A brand new Will, who'd left his old self behind in Vermont. I pulled him away from his sexy entourage.

"Will," I hissed in a whisper, "keep your mouth shut about your winnings, or these girls will strip you bare."

"They already have," he said, raising a confident eyebrow. Just like Will—he'd always been generous, never understood the meaning of money. "Have already stripped me, already stripped me."

"How much?" I said, wondering how he'd handle it when it finally sunk in what he'd done.

"All the way, sis. With all three." He was still grinning.

"Are you talking about what I think you're talking about?"

"Sure am."

"Did you use a condom?"

"I used three condoms."

I couldn't help but smile—Will always did take things literally. I had my answer, anyway. He was no longer a virgin. Three times no longer a virgin. "The money, have you spent it all?"

"Nooo, it's in the bank."

"In a bank? Like a *real* bank?"

"I opened up a bank account today. Put my winnings in, except I did buy the girls dresses, and drinks and, well . . . maybe some jewelry. Taking them out tonight, dresses and all. They look great in their dresses, great in their dresses."

"You put the money in a *bank?*"

"Better under a mattress? Or down a bra?" He laughed. I was reeling with this information; Will and banks didn't seem to go hand in hand.

"Will, how much are you talking about?"

"Eighty thousand dollars. Give or take, give or take, give or take."

"Holy shit! You're kidding me?"

"Nope."

"And you put it in a bank?"

"Yup."

I narrowed my eyes. "In your name, or in one

of the girl's names?"

"Janie, I'm not dumb." He twizzled around like Fred Astaire.

"Holy shit!" I sounded like a broken record. I hugged my not-so-little brother in celebration, my arms squeezing him in a tight embrace. Here I'd been thinking he needed my help. Maybe what he really needed, all along, was to get away from us— from Dad and me—to think clearly, be his own person, and this trip to Vegas offered that. We spoke some more and Will revealed that, before he laid his first bet on the table, he'd come up with an airtight plan; to quit after his third winning, put the money away, and only invest five percent with each new round. If he lost, he told me, too bad, but if he won, it would prove that his system worked. It did. Another thing he confided was that he'd planned this trip ahead of time.

Will was smarter than all of us put together.

"For now, just don't tell Dad, okay?" I suggested. "He's shell-shocked enough as it is with this whole . . . whole *manhood* thing, he doesn't need to know about the money yet. Just promise me you'll be careful, Will."

"I promise, I promise. I promise."

Just then my cell rang. Daniel.

"Did you find your brother?" he asked.

I told him the Will saga and he laughed.

"Have you been to your room?" he said. Just hearing Daniel's raspy voice was doing things to my body.

"No, why?"

"Because there's something waiting for you when you get there."

"Champagne?"

"No, I want you sober."

"What then?"

"Something for tonight. I'm taking you to a party."

"A party?" I instantly wondered if I had anything to wear.

"A Hollywood party at the Bellagio, a lot of producers and directors will be there."

"Are my father and Will invited?"

"If you want them to be, sure."

"Okay, I'll mull that one over."

"A show first, though, just us, no third party. If they want to come they can meet us later. I'll knock at your door around seven, Janie. Be ready."

"What's the show?"

"Something that will inspire a performer like you. You'll love it. See you at seven."

I LEFT WILL TO HIS GIRLS, and Dad by the bar, where he'd run into an old musician friend of his from his Jazz band days.

I dove into my room with excitement. A giant, very fancy shopping bag, with an equally enormous box inside, was lying seductively on the bed. I took the box out of the bag with both hands keeping it steady. I opened it up, discarding the silky ribbon, which I rolled up neatly and stuffed into a corner of my suitcase as a memento. Then I remembered to wash my hands—didn't want to sully the fabric of whatever was inside, not that my hands were dirty, but germs—any—were not welcome. Daniel's Howard Hughes's mania had gotten to me.

I had never been bought a dress before, except by my mom. My heart was drumming with antici-pation. *Why am I expecting a dress? It could be a pants suit or even a robe, or maybe not an article of clothing at all but a beach towel or something.*

But I was right: it was a dress. So exquisite, it brought tears to my eyes. Sleek, soft, supple, silky.

In a rich chocolate brown. It moved like flowing water when I held it against my body. The back was scooped, almost all the way down to the butt. Stunning. Sexy but elegant. Classy. All the things Daniel had told me that I was. The label was an expensive Italian brand—I knew so little about fashion. Then I panicked . . . *how does Daniel know my size? I'll be too embarrassed to tell him if it doesn't fit—things rarely do, especially around the bust.*

I envisioned myself at the party, swimming in this designer dress, my boobs on full view.

But when I slipped into it, it did fit. So perfectly, I wondered if Daniel had used Jake and Star's trick: calling the wardrobe department for my measurements. Then I noticed another bag nestled on the floor: Salvatore Ferragamo. I pulled out the box and opened it up: a pair of high, nude, peep-toe pumps. I eased my feet in slowly and stood up, trying not to teeter—I needed to practice walking a bit, especially in this dress. I was used to Converse trainers and wanted to look effortless in front of Daniel and all the Hollywood producers who would be at the party tonight.

4

THE SURPRISE SHOW was *O* by *Cirque du Soleil*, at the Bellagio. The best seats in the house. The entire stage was a swimming pool, and the act was replete with synchronized swimmers, Olympic-class divers, and acrobatic artists; the story unfolding above, below, and in the water. Daniel was right; nothing could have inspired me more than this breathtaking, surrealistic phenomenon, full of magical, dare-defying acts, and so many colors and imaginative forms, my head was spinning. Dancers painted like zebras, flashes of scarlet, turquoise, yellow, and blue reflected and bounced off the rippling pool, fire acts performing implausible feats. Pure theatrical romance engulfing us, transporting us into a dizzied reverie, making us forget that these were human beings doing the impossible. The show was one, extraordinary package of pure, unadulterated Art.

"Can you imagine doing five and a half flips?" I whispered in Daniel's ear, not averting my gaze from the acrobat spinning through the air, and flying downwards, before he hit the water in a graceful dive. Daniel didn't answer, just squeezed my hand. *Daniel and I are on a date!* A real *date*, I said to myself silently, over and over like a mantra.

No words passed between us after my comment, and when the finale came, with one of the performers playing a grand piano as it submerged into the glittering water—shimmering with lights and colors—I felt as if I had been transported to theatrical heaven: a place every actor loves to travel, to remind ourselves that make-believe and art really are important, and just because you aren't a doctor doesn't mean you aren't saving people's lives. Art is survival. This spectacle tonight was pure soul food.

"Thank you," I murmured in Daniel's ear, after we, the audience, had torn the house down with our claps and cheers.

"What for?"

"For nourishing my psyche—I needed that after my spate in Hollywood."

"You're so welcome. By the way, I can't do five and a half flips, but I can do two."

"You're kidding!"

"I'm a Leo, after all, I like showing off in front of pretty women. I'll show you when we go to Hydra this summer, there's a rock I like to dive off into the sea."

A thrill pricked every nerve in my body. "Greece? You're taking me to a *Greek island?*"

"If you'll come."

I gave him a mischievous eyebrow raise as if to say "maybe." Like hell. *You bet I will.*

I loved leaning against Daniel, as he held me steady in my heels, my arm linked in his. He was wearing a tux and was the epitome of handsome. We were a **couple**. Finally, after all this time, I felt my confidence blossom. We looked good together; I could tell by the way people dragged their gazes over us and then smiled, appreciating what they observed: a man and woman in love.

"I have a house there, that looks onto the Mediterranean. You'll love it."

"You're full of surprises, Daniel Glass. What

else haven't you told me about yourself?"

"You'll find out, bit by bit. But I hope you won't hold any of it against me."

"Like what?"

"Like . . . I'm a cricket fanatic."

I nearly said, *I know,* but sucked in my cheeks to stop myself, for fear of Daniel getting wind of my stalker tendencies.

"You play, or just watch?" I said instead.

"I'm on an English team. You can come and eat cream teas in pavilions, on lazy summer afternoons, while I run back and forth in white, boring you silly. Or you can get drunk on Pimms."

"What's Pimms?"

"An alcoholic drink with bits of cucumber and strawberries floating about in it. A rather disgusting, upper-crust summer drink that the British love."

I was feeling heady just talking about all these future plans. Daniel was into me. As in . . . *girl-friend/boyfriend* into me. I rested my head on his shoulder as we stepped into the elevator that would lead us up to the party. He eyed me up and down, his stare sexual, hungry. I could hear his measured breath. His hand trailed from the nape of my neck, down my flesh to the small of my back, and the tips of his cool fingers lodged themselves in between the elastic of my skimpy panties.

The car stopped at the fourth floor and two men got out, leaving us alone.

He whispered in my ear, "Love your dress, you're making me hard just looking at you." His hand traveled down and cupped my butt, letting his finger slip down my crack.

"*Daniel.*"

"I'm going to take this," —his voice was a rasp, low, and determined—"when you're ready."

I felt my face flush red, and pretended I hadn't heard him. Then I thought twice and said, "Maybe I never will be."

"Oh, you will be, trust me." He trailed his hand up my backbone, causing goose bumps to sprinkle all over my flesh, my nipples to harden. He tugged lightly on my hair so my chin tipped up, and with his other hand took mine—the one that wasn't holding my clutch purse—and pressed it against his groin. I gasped at his sudden dominance. I was pinned against the elevator car, his hand cupped over mine, as I felt his thick ridge between my fingers, through the fine fabric of his slacks.

"See what you do to me." His lips hovered over mine—even his breath was delicious.

"Oh God," I murmured, ready for his kiss. But the elevator doors suddenly opened and there we were, already at the party. I could hear voices and moneyed laughter. Glasses clinking, heels clicking. Will would be here with his girls. Not my dad, though, he'd told me he wanted to stay behind and catch up with his friend and his wife.

I felt so special walking into the room, dressed in our fine clothes, with Daniel holding my hand. The party was milling with beautiful people all schmoozing and networking. It spilled into several, separate rooms, champagne flowing, and handsome waiters and waitresses slipping in and out of the crowds with trays full of elaborate canapés. My gaze floated in a sort of daze over the famous faces of movie stars and sparkling jewelry, until my eyes landed in a surprised jolt on none other than Cal! He was with a pretty blonde, but said something to her before breaking away, as if he didn't want me to realize that they were together. *Too late, buster, I'm with Daniel now.* He inched his way toward me through the hustle of designer-clad bodies.

Daniel turned to me, "Janie, there's someone here I need to talk to. Boring shoptalk stuff. Won't be long." Daniel nodded in the direction of a group of CEO types.

"Oh," I said, disappointed. I wanted Cal to see us together, just to make a point. Daniel noticed my face as it fell into a disillusioned pout.

"You're a confident actress, pleasing crowds is your job." He winked at me. "Don't look so forlorn." He squeezed my hand and made his way to the other side of the room.

"Janie!" Cal said, coming up beside me. "Great to see you."

"I thought you were in Vancouver, filming." I gave him a wan smile and did the air kiss thing. He was also dressed in a tux and did look good, I had to admit.

"Doing a few days filming here, first. I know, it was a surprise to me, too."

"Who's the girl?" I wondered why I said that. It wasn't as if I cared, but I wanted to make Cal feel awkward after all those nice things he'd said to me, when it had obviously been bullshit. Thought I'd call him out on it."

"Nobody special, just an acquaintance." His gaze traveled from my head to my toe. "You look amazing, Janie, just beautiful."

"Thank you."

"I haven't forgotten our plans, by the way."

"Plans?" I said, as if I hadn't remembered.

"To drive up PCH, take a weekend together."

I shrugged. "Oh, I'd forgotten about that and thought you had too, with all the excitement of your new job."

He leaned in close to me and whispered, "How could I forget something like that? You look incredible, Janie . . ." –his eyes strayed to the other side of the room—"shit, is that Daniel Glass?" Cal's brow creased into a sharp frown.

"Yeah, actually, Cal, Daniel and I—"

"Fuck, is that the time?" –Cal glanced at his watch—"I've gotta meet someone. Bye, Janie, I'll call." He'd gotten the hint, obviously, that Daniel and I were an item. *Good.* Cal made a B-line out of the room, crushing through the sea of glamorous bodies. The blonde whom he'd been talking to met my eye and gave me a thin smile, so I took that as an invitation to say hi. Why not? I needed to mingle while Daniel was talking business.

She was pretty—very LA, in a tight little red dress, her cleavage beyond ample. Very "done" but done well, nonetheless.

"Daniel sure high-tailed it out of there," she remarked, her smile weak. "Hi, I'm Sydney."

I felt a little insulted by her 'Daniel' remark but just said, "business stuff, you know, he wanted to talk to some boring CEO types."

"He's a close friend of yours?" she pried, her eyes sizing me up and down as if to check out the competition.

"You could say that."

She cast her gaze downwards—I could see hurt flit across her face. I knew that Daniel was a magnet, and women loved him, but why the sad expression?

"We're seeing each other," I said, just to make things crystal clear. I wondered if this would be my new role; guard dog holding on to my territory. *Keep away from my man!*

Her eyes glistened as if she were about to burst out crying. "Oh, I had *no* idea—the asshole could have told me!"

"What?" I hissed, "you two have something going *on?*"

"I had hoped so. I mean, no . . . but . . . well yeah, we just made out."

I stood tall. "But Daniel's been with me all evening. We just arrived half an hour ago."

"We are talking about the same man, aren't we? Daniel Glass, the movie director?"

I looked across the other side of the room but couldn't see him.

"The guy you were just talking to five minutes ago?" she went on.

I frowned with confusion. "That was Cal. He's an actor. Cal Halpan."

"The dark-haired guy who just left in a hurry was Daniel Glass," she said emphatically.

"No, believe me, that was Cal Halpan. Daniel Glass is here, in another room, and he's my date, and the guy you made out with was *not* Daniel Glass, I can assure you."

"But he told me he was Daniel Glass!"

Everything began to fit into place. Cal must have been masquerading as Daniel and sweet-talking blond actresses into bed, or in this case, up against a wall somewhere. I got my cellphone out to show her photos on the web of Daniel, but remembered; they were few and far between, he was very private and didn't like the limelight. I scrolled through the ones I found but none of them were close-ups—no wonder Cal had gotten away with it—both men were tall, dark and handsome. I wanted to feel furious with Cal—this was identity theft! But I couldn't. Relief surged through me in a blissful wave, perhaps a smile was creeping across my face. Daniel had not been fucking his way around Hollywood, he'd been telling the truth!

I punched in Cal's number and handed Sydney my phone. "You speak to Cal. Tell him he's been busted and his little game makes him look like a real jerk."

She snatched my phone but pressed the red button to end the ringtone. "No," she said, "I think I've been humiliated enough—don't want to rub salt into my wound. I just don't get why—"

"*Your* wound? It's Cal who should feel humiliated!" I said. "Pretty sad and pathetic, I'd say, to go around impersonating someone else, especially as he doesn't need to. And *especially* when the person he's mimicking has orchestrated a plum role for him in a TV series. What an a-hole!"

A waiter came by, and I popped a canapé into my mouth. It was delicious. Sydney stepped closer, her breasts nestling up against my arm. "He made me do an audition for him," she whispered conspiratorially, "for the movie, *The Dark Edge of Love*." Her whisper was laced with whimsical desire. *She was still into him, even after knowing he was a total fraud?*

"What did he make you do?" I asked, my curiosity piqued.

"Put it this way . . . tomorrow I'll have a bunch of bruises all over me, especially on my butt."

I raised my eyebrows. "Playing Dom, was he? I'm so sorry he did that to you." I felt badly for her, but her stupidity stunned me. I added, "The part in *The Dark Edge of Love* is mine, by the way—it's not up for grabs."

I suddenly realized what I'd said; *the part is mine*. I hadn't signed the deal yet, but I was damned if any other actress would be getting close up and personal with Daniel. The real Daniel. I still could not believe what Cal had been playing at.

"Sydney, I'm sorry you got hoodwinked by Cal. What he did is beyond dishonorable, it's cheap!"

To my amazement she replied, "But I really like him, and he's so hot, it could have been worse."

"Oh, okay, so I shouldn't feel badly for you, then? Not furious on behalf of the female sex? Even after he totally lied to you?"

Her cheeks flushed. She wasn't a Natasha Jürgen lookalike, after all—she couldn't have been more than twenty-two and didn't have the poise and sophistication of Daniel's late wife. Jake and Star had gotten the gossip wrong, this woman was one hundred percent Hollywood fodder: lacking in brain cells, although fabulous to look at. In a babelicious sort of way. No wonder men like Cal got away with behaving like this, when women like Sydney were so readily available. And gullible.

"Yeah, I really, really like him," she admitted.

I shrugged my shoulders. *To each their own.* "Hey, if you like him, call him."

Her eyes brightened. "You think I have a chance?"

I stood there, open-mouthed. Then I said, "Who knows? Give it a go. And while you're at it, tell him to stop pretending he's someone else, especially when that someone is my . . . my boyfriend."

Renewed hope glittered in Sydney's big round

eyes. I left her to her fate and found Daniel in another room, deep in conversation, talking shop with some money people.

After introducing me to the group as his 'girlfriend and number one leading lady' Daniel took my hand. "I'm done, Janie, I hope you weren't hit on too many times."

The 'girlfriend' label had my head spinning. All I could think of was consummating our union. "I'd like to go back to where we left off," I told him.

"The elevator?" His mouth curled into a wicked smile.

"No, before that. In the airplane. I think I'm brave enough to handle you now." *We all know what I'll be handling.*

I whispered in his ear, "I'd like to start rehearsing for the movie."

Relief flooded his face. "Is that a yes, then? You'll do the part of Sylvie?"

I nuzzled my head against the lapel of his tux. "It's a yes, in every single way possible."

He took me by the hand and, with his other resting on the small of my back, led me away from the crowded party. The buzz of being Daniel's official girlfriend sent tingles all over my body. A grin spread from one ear to the other.

"You seem to have a definite purpose, where are you taking me?" I asked him.

"Gambling."

"*Gambling?*"

"Don't sound so shocked, Janie, we're in Vegas after all."

For some reason I'd assumed we'd be going to his hotel to celebrate, and in my fantasies the kind of celebration had to do with getting stark naked and frolicking between the sheets, or anywhere else he had in mind. Gambling hadn't been part of my plan. Not at all.

"I've never gambled before and I don't want to start now," I complained, hoping he'd change his mind. I thought of Will winning all that money and wondered why I hadn't seen him at the party.

"You don't have to," Daniel said. "Just hang onto my arm, choose a number, and be my lucky mascot." I loved the idea of hanging on his arm but dreaded the moment when he lost because of the dud numbers I might pick.

"Are we going far?" I was tottering in my heels and my feet were beginning to ache.

"No. Right here in the Bellagio. Not bad to have a show, a party, and gambling all under one roof. Also, there's a European wheel here, which is a single 0 wheel, rather than the 00 wheel, so we have more chance of winning. The house edge on the single 0 wheel is just over two and a half percent, whereas on the 00 roulette wheel, the American wheel, the house edge doubles to over five and a half percent. Hence sticking with this casino."

"Jeez, it sounds like you're a professional, I didn't know there were nerd gamblers."

The corner of his lip quirked up, and he pressed the button for the elevator. "I just dabble when the mood takes me."

We got into the elevator car and I couldn't hold it in any longer. "Daniel, something kind of unpleasant happened at the party."

His eyes bored into me. "I knew I shouldn't have left you alone, but I thought you'd have more fun chatting up movie stars than listening to boring money talk about investments, mergers and take-overs. Don't tell me I'm going to have to punch someone out?"

"Well, yeah, maybe you should."

His eyes darkened. "Mild flirtation or gross behavior, because if it was the latter, I won't be happy. Not one bit."

"Cal," I said. "He's running around Hollywood and Vegas pretending he's you, telling people his name is Daniel Glass."

To my astonishment, Daniel roared with laughter.

"It's not funny! You've got a reputation now as a womanizer . . . that's why I thought you were shagging Natasha Jürgen lookalikes."

"And to think I gave him that job. He shouldn't bite the hand that feeds."

"Exactly," I agreed.

"He must be pretty screwed up to think he can get away with it."

"Well what are you going to do about it?" We arrived at the casino, Daniel rested his hand on my behind and steered me out of the elevator. I loved this new Daniel, the Daniel who was keen to show in public that I belonged to him.

"Nothing," he said. "Let him have his fun. There's one thing you should know about me; I don't give a fuck what people think. I know who I am, and if my friends doubt me or judge me, then they're not my friends and they can fuck right off. Let's go and play. You ready?"

"Don't blame me if I lose."

"I'd never blame you for anything, Janie. Come. Something tells me tonight's going to be pretty interesting."

There were no seats at the roulette table, but an elderly man made way for us to get in on the action. There was a lighted board that indicated the last winning numbers. Daniel noticed me studying it.

"Don't pay attention to that," he warned. "That's how they make their money. Every roulette play is completely random and has nothing to do with previous wins. Just because black came up the last seven times doesn't necessarily mean red is due to come up next. Ever heard of the law of independent trials?"

I shook my head. More evidence that Daniel was steeped in this dangerous world. At least he had the money to experiment with his dollars. Could *afford* to take risks.

"If most people see one color come up several times in a row, the odds are they'll bet the opposite color, and lose," he explained.

He took out a wad of freshly minted hundred dollar bills from his jacket pocket and bought several stacks of chips. I wanted to run from the casino, there and then. I felt sick to my stomach at the thought of anyone losing all that money, especially on my account.

The croupier spun the wheel and called out, "Ladies and gentlemen, place your bets."

"Go ahead, Janie," Daniel urged.

"I know nothing about this game," I said in a low voice, my heart in my throat.

"Pick a number, pick a color. Quick."

"Okay, black and nineteen," I said on impulse. I was nineteen when I lost my virginity, and for some reason, at this present moment, I had sex on the brain. Perhaps it was because everything that Daniel did was sexy; the way he moved, the way he challenged me with his azure eyes—his dark, mussed up hair, his wicked smile, his confidence. But mostly, the flashbacks of what had happened in the plane, the memory of how huge he was and how much he'd desired me.

Daniel placed a high pile of chips on 19 and some on various other numbers, his long fingers cool and unhurried. My eyes moved with the ball as it clunked over several different numbers on the spinning wheel. I immediately wished I'd picked red and the number 15, my lucky number. I felt as if time was frozen as everyone's locked gazes followed the little white ball tumbling over one number to the next. Finally it landed on 15, and I felt completely nauseous. *I knew it, I knew it!* But then, like magic, it toppled over into the 19 slot. I waited, holding my breath. What if it toppled over again into the next number and we lost?

But it didn't. I gasped, my heart racing a million miles an hour. I thought I'd faint again, the way I had before I'd ended up in the hospital. But Daniel had me in his grasp, his hands clinched around my waist, as if he knew instinctively how shocked I'd be.

I squealed out in delight, and a few people at the table smiled at me. The croupier handed Daniel several colored chips.

"This one's for you, Janie," Daniel said, handing me a pretty pink and blue chip. I stared at it, stunned. It was worth $25,000!

"Don't be silly," I protested. I slipped it into his jacket pocket. But he retrieved it.

"It's yours. You're the one who picked the

winning number." He prized my clutch from my fingers, snapped it open and popped the pretty chip inside. "Just don't lose your purse," he warned. "And I'd cash it in soon, if I were you."

I opened my mouth to speak but thought of my student loan debt, and closed it again.

"Let's go," he said, "I don't want you getting hooked on this shit."

"Where are we going?"

"To my hotel. That is if what you said about rehearsing was true."

I could feel heat rise to my face. *Rehearsing for the movie. Playing the BDSM game.* Hmm, the idea sent shivers along my bare spine.

Daniel pulled me away from the table, nodding a thank you to the croupier and tipping him. He said quietly, "Janie, are you *sure* you're up for it?" He looked at his watch. "It's nearly midnight."

I rolled my eyes. "I'm not Cinderella."

"I haven't fed you, you need to eat something first."

"I stuffed myself with hors d'oeuvres at the party," I fibbed. I hadn't. Was too excited to eat, I simply didn't have an appetite.

"You really want me to get into character?"

I felt that familiar Daniel ache between my legs. "Yeah, I do."

"As *Finn*?"

I giggled. "You make him sound like Dr. Jekyll and Mr. Hyde."

Daniel didn't smile. "We don't know yet what he's capable of."

He, not Daniel himself, I noticed. Ever the actor.

"Finn's not going to turn into some serial killer, is he?" I joked.

But Daniel's face was solemn. "I don't know, Janie. I may want to . . . "—and he lowered his voice so only I could hear—"really go for it, you know. I don't trust myself if I had you in my room in private, with all those sex toys we have in the film. I've never done this 'Dom' shit before, I might get carried away."

"But we'll be doing it on set, anyway. Might as well start now."

"But it won't be *real* on set—we'll be acting. We'll have the crew around us."

"I want to try it out for real, though."

By now we had exited the hotel and were standing outside the Bellagio. The fountain light show was just beginning its extraordinary display: thousands of spritzers shooting hundreds of feet into the air, making synchronized dancing patterns on the large lake, which spanned several acres and separated the hotel from the Strip. Frank Sinatra's "Fly Me To The Moon" was playing. The water was glittering, Vegas beckoning, making me feel that everything and anything was possible. Risks paid off—didn't we just win all that money? It was now-or-never time. You only-live-once time. And I was definitely in the mood to fly to the moon with Daniel. Hell, I'd go with him anywhere. Yes, even Hell. I wanted him in every way possible, and in that moment, I needed him to own me in some way. To be his possession.

Daniel winced, then stopped walking. His tongue slid languidly along his top lip. "Oh fuck, Janie, you've made me hard discussing all this." I looked down at his crotch. There it was, that huge great ridge again, straining against his slacks. I could feel a slickness in my panties—it wasn't just Daniel getting excited in the nether regions.

"I want to *play*," I cajoled, slipping my arm under his dress shirt, and onto his warm, hard stomach, "experiment a bit, try it out for real and see what it's like—you know, do the Method."

The Method, started by Stanislavski and favored by actors like Marlon Brando, Dustin Hoffman, and Robert de Niro—the practice of connecting to a character by drawing on real emotions and memories, aided by a set of exercises and practices, including sense memory. But also living out the scenario for real, if possible. *Be* it, not just imagine it. *Be* the real thing, *do* the real thing, like De Niro putting on all that weight for *Raging Bull*—the Method in its extreme.

"It'll be more realistic if I actually *experience* it— at least once," I coaxed.

"You read the script, Janie. He whips her, ties her up, fucks her when she can't fend for herself, when she can't even move!"

"Yes, but they have a 'safe-word,' remember? If things get too rough, she calls out. I can do that if I don't like it, if you go too far."

Daniel shook his head, "We'll be playing with fire."

"What? *You're* the fire?" I laughed. "You can snuff out the flames anytime."

He laid his hand on the bulge of his pants— the evidence of how turned on he was, thick and full. "You see this? This is how you make me feel. All. The. Fucking. Time. I don't know what it is, Janie, but you get me really worked up. You saw what happened in the plane? No. No way, you're too vulnerable, too—"

"That was before you confessed to me about Natasha," I pointed out, my hand feeling the softness of his flesh, circling his taut waist. "In my mind you were still in love, still crazy about her. Now I know you love *me*, it'll be totally different. Plus, there's evidence that you haven't been screwing your way around Hollywood. Now I know that it was Cal, all along, not you. I feel more confident now. It's a completely different situation."

Daniel screwed up his face in thought and then relented, "Okay, we'll make a deal." He lowered his voice and looked around. Nobody was near us, and everyone was staring at the fountains, not noticing us in the least, but his voice was conspiratorial, low, and husky. "I'll fuck you first. Rough sex. No mercy." He turned my body to face him full on, and pulled me into his chest. He murmured, "I'll fuck you senseless, Janie. And if you can handle my hot Italian blood and my ruthless Viking madness that make up my unfortunate

DNA, *then* we can play act, okay?"

His words alone were driving me wild, not to mention his massive hard-on.

"Deal," I agreed. His erection dug into my belly—his height making me feel small and fragile. He took my face into his hands and held my gaze, before he kissed me firmly on the mouth. It was a kiss that spoke of a sealed deal, a pact.

There was no going back now.

5

WE HADN'T SPOKEN since that moment, not verbally anyway. The atmosphere was charged with sex, the heat between us near to boiling point—we needed no actual words to communicate. We were on our way back to his hotel, driving in his ginormous private limo, the chauffeur not able to see us because of the privacy divider, but by now, I was a little nervous, because Daniel had instructed him that we were not to be disturbed. What had he in mind?

"Bend," Daniel murmured in a dominant tone, his lips grazing over the shell of my ear, sending delicious shivers along my spine, right to my toes. "I need to take off your dress. Wait," he breathed into my neck, "first, let me rid you of your shoes."

I laid back into the sumptuous bench seat as he slid the high pumps off my aching feet, Daniel on his knees. Then he leaned back, in quiet perusal of my face and body, his eyes now provocatively heavy-lidded, raking me up and down until they lingered on my mouth, before settling back to my hungry gaze.

"Fuck, you're beautiful, Janie. Unusually beautiful."

"So are you," I answered. His dark hair, as always, was slightly wayward, and his luminous blue eyes flecked with black. Avaricious, determined. I had his attention one hundred percent, and I reveled in it. All that time, when we were working together, I had fantasized about this moment: Daniel wanting me, craving my touch, desperate to fuck me. My mouth parted, letting in the oxygen that I needed not to pass out. This man I was so hopelessly in love with had just told me I was beautiful, and it was clear he wanted to eat me alive.

And I wanted to be eaten.

He pulled the top of my dress so my shoulders were bare. It shimmied down, landing in a silky pool around my waist. My breasts exposed, my nipples rosy and erect. He leaned over, his warm breath on my collarbone, where he planted a wet kiss. I was waiting to be ravaged, the way he had promised me, waiting for the dark Viking to rip me in two until I couldn't walk properly, but so far, Daniel seemed reverent, respectful, as if I were a China doll.

But lust was shimmering in his eyes—dark—Prussian blue now, like a stormy ocean where I could drown. The lights of the Strip flickered by the moving car, although the tinted windows of the limo kept us safe from prying eyes. But reds and golden yellows lit up Daniel's intent, undistracted face. All concentration was on me, and me alone. He took off his tailored jacket, unbuttoned his shirt, pulled his shirttails from the waistband of his trousers, took off his silver cufflinks, and stuffed them in his pocket. As smoothly as the cufflinks were slipped into his pocket, a foil packet was picked out. He undid his slacks, letting them drop, and tore off his boxer briefs, all in the space of seconds, not minutes. His beautiful body, all glory before my eyes, his huge cock rising toward his navel had me ripping off my panties—soaked as they were—and hitching up my dress. I whimpered, solely at the anticipation of having his thick, hard cock inside me. Our eyes were connected; he hadn't let his gaze leave mine for one moment.

I opened my legs and squirmed on the seat.

"Wider," he commanded, his lusty gaze straying down to my glistening pussy. He licked his lips. His cock was proud, smooth as glass, yet intimidating.

I thought he was going to perform oral sex, but still kneeling, Daniel splayed my legs wider apart and swiftly entered me, groaning as he drove in, in one hard, long stroke. His knees forcing my legs wide, his hands holding mine, pushing them out so I was like a starfish—all his.

"Oh . . . Daniel."

He groaned and squeezed his eyes shut as if the pleasure was almost unbearable. "Feels amazing, doesn't it?" His lips were then on mine, as he fucked me and kissed me at the same time, his hips pumping into me rhythmically, his rock-hard cock thrusting in and out of me. I needed this so much.

Then he stilled. I could feel him throbbing inside me like a heartbeat. I knew what he was doing; trying to pace himself, but the rhythmic pulse of his thickness, the solidity of it filling my walls, his intense eyes on mine, with a look of love flickering in his irises, drew a mind-blowing orgasm out of me before I realized what was happening.

I started squirming and crying out as the climax coursed through me so unexpectedly, Daniel's hands holding mine down so I couldn't even touch him, his hips still, but the girth of his cock expanding, so huge and deep inside me, touching every sensitive nerve, his wet heat exploding.

He let out a low guttural groan. "Oh Janie, you see what you do to me?" His words entered my mouth like a secret, the sounds on his breath an arrow to my soul.

"What we do to *each other*," I murmured, my body pounding with beautiful spasms of ecstasy.

He laughed quietly. "That was fast."

"You came at the same time?" My body was trembling.

"Course. That was fucking sexy what you did, Janie: your sounds, you so wet and tight . . . and gripping me like that. Coming simultaneously isn't something every couple can do, so why hold back? You and I are obviously hotwired."

Every couple. Hmm, I love that. Hotwired. I'll say.

"I . . . it's never happened like this before."

"We're just warming up, baby, there's more where that came from—don't worry, I'm ready to go again."

"Me too," I said, surprising even myself. I wanted more of this addictive drug.

He pulled out of me, tore off the condom, knotted it, and let it drop on the carpeted floor. I noticed he was still hard. "I'm clean as a whistle, by the way—to use your expression. I got tested after I found out my wife had been cheating on me, and contrary to Hollywood gossip, I haven't been screwing around. I really hate using these things and I don't have another one on me, anyway, so if it's all right with you . . . " He buried his face in my neck and breathed me in like I was the most desirable, delicious thing in the world.

The idea of his bare flesh inside me sent another wave of desire shimmying through my core. But I told him, "I'm not on the pill." The truth was, if I'd gotten pregnant with Daniel, I wouldn't have even cared. On the contrary, I'd have been thrilled, but I wanted to be honest.

In one swift movement Daniel turned me

around, and maneuvered me on all fours. He cupped his hand neatly around my mound, the heel of his palm pressing hard against my sensitive opening, and the tips of his fingers on my clit. I pushed into his hand, mini orgasmic aftershocks causing tingles that made me hungry for more. If he kept this up I'd come again.

"Janie . . . Christ . . . this view . . . your ass, your pretty wet cunt so ready for me again . . . *so* fucking sexy."

His fingers trailed my wetness from between my thighs up along my butt crack, where he massaged me slowly, deliberately, circling my opening, lubricating it with my arousal.

"Relax, Janie, this part of you is just as beautiful and delicious as the rest."

The next thing I knew I sensed his tongue exploring that clandestine part of me. Relief that I'd thoroughly showered, earlier, flooded some part of my sex-numbed brain, because the feeling was so exquisite, so illicit and naughty, that I couldn't deny this newfound pleasure. Daniel was growling with enjoyment, which turned me on even more. This was wrong, wasn't it? Like animals we were, me in the doggie position. But Daniel didn't let up, his tongue probed inside me, his spittle lubricating me even more, teasing me, like a flower bud being forced open. I felt a sudden fullness and became aware of his thumb slipping inside, fitting like a warm welcome. I couldn't believe how good it felt. He thumb-fucked me, easing it in and out, spreading his spittle inside, swirling it gently around until this invasion of something foreign to me felt completely normal. No pain, just an overwhelming sensation of fullness. At the same time, he kept up the pressure of his fingers on my clit—it was almost too much. Too much going on at once for my heightened senses.

"I think I'm going to come soon," I murmured.

"I should hope so," he rumbled. "You want more of this? You want it all?"

"All?"

"I need to claim this ass, Janie. I won't be a hundred percent satisfied until I can call every last centimeter of your body mine. Call me greedy, I am." I could feel the rod of his erection against my thigh; his whopping great dangerous tool that could undo me—maybe cause me acute pain.

"Try me," I threw out, bucking rhythmically to

the intrusion of his thumb, and rocking against his hand."

"You're sure you're ready?"

I moaned in response.

"I'll give you just a taste, see how we go. Just the tip of my cock, but I warn you, you're so fucking hot I could come all over you, come inside you."

"Please," I groaned.

When he took out his thumb, a needy pounding had me silently begging for all of him. I was scared, tremulous, but thrilled, even my erotic dreams hadn't taken me this far with Daniel.

He grabbed my ass with both hands and brought me closer to him. Then I felt his wide crest, lubricated with his pre-cum, probe at my gateway; a gateway to pure pleasure. Or agony? I'd have to find out. My heart was beating a trillion miles an hour.

He entered me a millimeter.

"More," I moaned.

"Oh, fuck, Janie." He pushed himself in a little more, and I sensed that wicked fullness again, but this time the feeling far greater, almost depraved.

"You've done this before?" I asked him, my

voice a tremor. I hoped he knew what he was doing.

"No. Never. Never felt the need before. But I *have* to have you, Janie. All of you. Every last inch. This is a treasure chest and I want to be the first, and last, to open it up."

The thought that he hadn't done this with anyone else made my heart swell with happiness. I had conquered him. *She* hadn't elicited this level of desire. This filthy, bad, dirty-driven man was *mine*.

"How do you know you're the first?" I teased.

"Because I'm the only one who's got the right key," he said with confidence, his voice gruff.

He eased himself in a fraction more.

"Okay?" he asked. I could, for a second, feel a sharp stab, but soon it dulled and I wanted more. More of Daniel Glass. More of his cutting pain.

"Don't stop," I said. He desired all of me? The feeling was mutual.

"*Have* to have you, Janie. Every . . . —" he thrust in deeper—"Last . . . "—deeper still—"Millimeter." He punctuated each word with his movements, pushing in slowly—a feeling so alien, I couldn't even place it. Not seeing his face was unnerving. All I knew, though, was I didn't want him to stop. He was gripping my buttocks like they belonged to him, his cock delving into my secret place, deeper, more taboo, on every thrust. But then, as if by osmosis, knowing what my body needed, Daniel brought his hand to my clit and began to rub, cupping my entire mound with the strength of his whole palm, draping over and around me like a magic glove, pressing all the right buttons.

I entered into a new realm. A tunnel of flashing lights. But the pleasure . . . dark. Forbidden.

"Oh . . . fuck," I moaned.

Each thrust was coupled with his hand gripping my core, building, building into a monument of painful gratification. Yes, it hurt back there, I couldn't deny it. But in a good way . . .

Pain. And pleasure. Pleasure. And pain.

Opposites melding into one whole.

"This. Hot. Little. Ass. Is. Going. To. Make. Me. Fucking well detonate!" Daniel was trailing kisses all over my back, lashing his tongue on my flesh, that skillful hand still cupping me tight, my clit rippling in a delicious, delirious world of its own.

"I'm coming," I screamed out, hoping the limo

was soundproof and, just after I said it, I could feel Daniel's fountain of wet heat shoot into me, literally a millisecond after I fell to pieces with the strangest, yet most powerful orgasm of my life.

Perfect timing, once again.

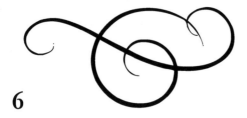

6

"**Y**OU SURPASSED YOURSELF, Miss Cole," Daniel said, a trace of a smile passing across his face.

We were back at the apartment of his swanky hotel that had floor to ceiling windows, which looked out to the colorful Vegas lights and to the horizon beyond. He had carried me here—both of us in a semi-state of undress—riding the elevator to his penthouse, as he carried my worn body in his arms, across the threshold, straight to the bathroom where I was now, soaking gloriously in a white marble hot tub. He'd ordered room service, earlier, watching me as I ate a bowl of pasta while in the bath. I now felt exhausted, spent, both physically and mentally. He'd pushed my limits.

And I'd let him.

I didn't reply to his comment. He had just gotten out of the shower and, leaning over me with his dripping wet hair, planted a chaste kiss on my forehead. He knew better than to tamper further with my boundaries and he could, perhaps, gauge my silent mood. There was a part of me that felt angry with him, as if I had given him a little piece of my soul that he might take and store in a dark place, never to return it. As if he were a vampire drinking my blood. He'd stolen something from me tonight.

"It was a one-off," I replied in a quiet voice.

"That's fine, baby. Just great to know we have that bond and belong to each other now. We melded in a very meaningful way, don't underestimate the significance of what we did."

Melded. That was the very word I had thought of. There was no doubt that Daniel was right. I lifted my chin. "I don't belong to anyone, Daniel. And I'm not your baby." Why I said this, I had no idea. I wanted to claim my independence, prove to him that I was my own person, not weak-willed, not his toy. I wanted him to believe I didn't need him. I was begging myself to believe that too.

"Kate, with her shrew-like claws out, I see," he said, referring to the role he always said I should play: Kate from *Taming of the Shrew*. Daniel chuckled, almost enjoying my mercurial disposition that less than an hour ago had me in such a vulnerable yet wanton place—all his; every single part of me—but now had me taking back my power. Or trying to. He loved a challenge.

"Watch out or these claws could strike," I murmured.

"I think it's your bed time." He stood up and fetched a giant, fluffy towel from a heater rack and helped me out of the tub. I stood there like a child as he patted me dry, my lips set in a sullen pout. The man had taken me, pulled out an illicit orgasm from my body as if it were the easiest most natural thing in the world. I should have been rejoicing to feel so in love with him, so at one, but all I wanted to do was fight. Rebel. Kick and scream.

But not tonight. I was too tired. He'd worn me down. He'd taken everything from me and was calling it his own.

And I hated him for it.

I WAS AWOKEN by Daniel's kiss, soft on my

lips, and inhaled his Glassy scent, which mingled with the tail end of my dreams . . . a cliff, me flying, an angel . . . I was still immersed in my fantasy world. Light accosted my face, but I kept my eyes firmly closed. I wasn't ready to get up yet, and feeling too just-fucked—even though it happened hours ago—to have more sex with him right now.

"Beautiful girl," he whispered. "Beautiful, beautiful girl."

I heard him quietly leave the room and make a couple of phone calls, the second of which caught my attention.

As if he were ordering takeout, he rattled off a list of sex toys to buy, some of which sounded more like torture implements from the medieval age.

"Yes, some handcuffs, but nice ones, you know, lined with something soft so they don't bruise the wrists. What else . . . let me think . . . Oh yes, a set of . . .um . . . nipple clamps."

My ears perked up. Nipple clamps? *Ouch.*

"A couple of whips, one with a tassel, and a riding crop one."

Double ouch.

"And a paddle for spanking."

Triple ouch, but very, very curious.

"A bondage scarf, or mask, or whatever looks sexy, but also a little dangerous."

Hmm, yes.

"Edible body paint, or maybe just some sort of melted chocolate." *Oh, yes please.*

"Black, lace, crotchless panties, and bra to match . . . better be extra small," he added as an afterthought.

Wait, hang on . . . that's a bit intimate . . . who the hell is he speaking to anyway? One of his minions? Daniel was used to people running around for him. Embarrassing . . . I only hoped I didn't have to come face to face with this person.

I lay there, still half dreaming, too tired from last night to get up. Daniel obviously had more kinky stuff planned and, despite my cross face, mock rebellion, and threat of claws, I now welcomed 'playtime' with relish. *Rehearsals, here we come!* I couldn't wait. I'd always loved working with Daniel, but this would be the most thrilling experience of all.

I slipped back into slumber, expecting Daniel to wake me in an hour or so.

But when I did finally haul myself out of bed, he was gone.

The smell of freshly brewed coffee stirred my senses. I found a note by the coffee machine.

Janie,

I saw the fire in your eyes last night after our extraordinary tryst. I can only see what happened as a beautiful thing, and it seemed you loved every second of it, although I fear you now feel compromised in some way. I admit, it seemed like an act of domination on my part, of male conquest. But it was more than that. Far more. **"Love is composed of a single soul inhabiting two bodies."** Aristotle said that, and it's true.

Janie, I cannot deny I want each tiny part of you to be mine. You inspire me in a way no woman has. Ever. You desire me in a way that no woman has. Ever. I was a broken man and you are piecing me together, little by little. Shattered pieces of Daniel Glass, that's who I was . . .I had lost all faith in women, all trust, and you, Janie, have given me hope.

Let me show you all the ways I can love you.

Don't eschew the inevitable.

Because it is . . . inevitable . . .

You. And. Me.

Me. And. You.

Always yours,

Daniel

P.S. I'm out for the day. I have business to attend to and a little space does always seem to make the heart grow fonder. And I'm sure you'll secretly miss me.

P.P.S. Took the liberty of ordering a few props for our "rehearsal." I do believe, Miss Cole, after the way you so obviously enjoyed our scenario in the limo, you're definitely ready for more, even if

you are sharpening those shrew-like claws.
Your bites and scratches won't faze me
one bit, though. In fact, I rather relish
the idea of a bit of S&M.

Clever man. He always knew the right moment to hold back. Not having him here, not having him in my face alarmed me.

What 'business?' Where had he gone? Why couldn't he be more specific? I held the note in my hands, my pulse racing. *"Inevitable." "Domination." "Shattered pieces of Daniel Glass."* The words he chose were somehow shocking. It was true, he *had* been shattered by Natasha's cheating. Shattered too, I supposed, by her death, even if they were about to get divorced, even though he'd known the baby wasn't his.

Daniel loved me. Why did this terrify me? Would I lose myself in him completely if I submitted? Too late, I *had* submitted. This man was a powerhouse in every way. Persuasive, dominating. He could own me completely if I wasn't careful.

It was easy to revere someone from afar. Easy, when Daniel had been unattainable. But knowing the feeling was now mutual, and the relationship was changing from distant adoration to reciprocal, the present dynamic threw everything I had come to know out of balance.

And I had been so obsessed with Daniel for so long, and put him on such a high pedestal—used to being in a position of unrequited love—that now that true love was being offered to me—our relationship on an equal footing—I was flabbergasted.

Mainly because when something seems too good to be true, it usually is.

AFTER SHOWERING I called room service and ordered a hearty breakfast of cereal, toast, eggs, and hash browns. And fresh orange juice to wash it all down. I was ravenous. Daniel had depleted me. It had been that way in rehearsals for *As The Wind Blows*, too. His exacting, demanding character never letting up for a minute. His intense, blue-eyed gaze always on me, as if judging me, sizing me up. And now that there was sex in the equation, it was even harder to hold my own. My resolve of fighting for my independence was already waning. The ache between my legs, the throb of wanting him inside me, holding me in his arms, his breath on my face, his tongue in my mouth, had already picked up pace. And it wasn't even midday.

I replayed the limo scene in my mind and heard a low wistful whimper coming from my throat. I needed this man, for better or worse.

And boy, was I ready to start "rehearsals."

My cellphone caught me out of my reverie. It was Will. What had he done last night? It didn't bear thinking about, but I needed to let him have his freedom. Even if he was my little brother, Will was now twenty-one, and had shown us that he had a mind of his own. He was a man now—his body alone, not to mention his sexual appetite— had turned him into a new person.

"Will, what happened last night, how come you never showed?"

"I did, but you'd gone. You'd gone. Janie. Your guy's name is Daniel Glass, right? Right? The director you like? The director? The one who bought you that dress and took you to the party?"

"Yeah," I said, my voice tentative.

"The fuck!" Will shouted. "I met a couple blondes who told me—"

"No, Will, it's all gossip, don't believe—"

"How could he do that to you?"

"Will! Listen, it's all . . . Will, are you there? Hello . . ooo?" But he'd hung up.

I called my father. It took him a while to pick up. My gaze wandered to the Strip from the penthouse window: cars passing, people wandering in an out of hotels and casinos, the bright lights and neon signs of Vegas twinkling and flashing, the pale purple mountains in the distance, reminding you that this was nothing more than a massive patch of uncompromising desert.

"Janie," Dad said breathlessly. "Great to hear your voice. How was the party? Are you in your room, I'll come over. Or we can meet for breakfast, by the pool."

"I . . . " –I was a big girl, there was no reason why I should pretend that I'd spent the night in my room—that I had not been at Daniel's—but I found it hard to come out and say it. "Sure, but I have a few things to do first, how about lunch instead? Is Will with you?"

"No, he just went out in a rush but will be back later."

"Where did he go?"

"I have no idea, but seemed pissed at something. Janie, Will is taking on a whole other persona now, taking things into his own hands—it's all new to me, and I don't know how to handle it."

"I know, but I guess we have to let him be his own person."

"He's just a boy," he said, "just my little boy."

"I'll call you around noon and we can grab a bite to eat and have a chat about all this, okay?"

But lunch never happened. Just as I was walking out the door, my cell rang. It was the Vegas police.

Both Daniel and Will were in the hospital.

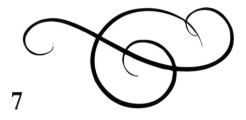

7

"WHAT THE HELL HAPPENED?" My eyes were so full of tears, I could hardly see. Will was lying in the hospital bed; one leg elevated in a contraption, an arm encased in a sling, and his split lips the size of a bruised peach, his jaw maroon and purple. Frankenstein stitches along his jaw. They had refused to let me in to see Daniel. He was in ER. Plus, I wasn't next of kin.

"I'm orry, anie. orry, orry." Will could hardly move his mouth.

I came up to his bed. He was in a sad state, but at least he was able to communicate, at least he was conscious.

"Why?" I wailed, hardly able to form a sentence. "Why couldn't you have just waited for me to explain?"

"Aniel's a 'ollywood player."

"You got the wrong guy, Will! Mistaken identity! Not a player, actually. And I can fight my own battles, I don't need . . ."—my breath hitched up an octave, I sucked in some air to get the sentence out —"my younger brother acting like a crazed vigilante on my behalf!" I was too upset to have this conversation. The damage had been done: Daniel was in 'Neuro, ICU' on life support, in a coma. And they wouldn't let me see him. I was a nobody as far as the hospital was concerned, with no rights whatsoever because I wasn't family.

I collapsed on a chair and sobbed my heart out, my body convulsing in heaving waves. Will lay there motionless, bandaged like a mummy, doing no more than flinching, his mouth finding it hard to form words because of the obvious pain he was in—all I heard were his low moans.

But it had been an accident, they'd told me. One so crazy it might have featured in a Charlie Chaplin movie, or some slapstick comedy. One of the police officers had explained to me what eyewitnesses saw: Will flying at Daniel in the lobby of one of Daniel's hotels, Will's fists flailing.

Floors that had just been polished to a high sheen. Daniel, not having ever met Will and taken by surprise, instinctively lashing out, his right leg kicking high in some martial arts move, catching Will hard under the jaw. Will flying through the air, Daniel's leather-soled dress shoes losing purchase as he slipped backwards on the shiny surface, his head catching on the corner of a table and smashing on the marble floor. Will crashing onto his side, crushing his hip and arm on the marble, and breaking his leg in two places, his arm very badly sprained.

Daniel unconscious, his head bleeding—concussion—followed by a coma, an hour later.

History repeating itself: Natasha Jürgen dying from a silly fall. Would that happen to Daniel, too?

It didn't bear thinking about.

His name was Daniel Glass. He was broken.

And I didn't have the power to fix him.

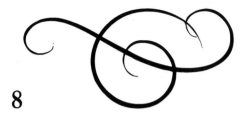

8

I HADN'T PLANNED on making Las Vegas my home, but there was no way I was going anywhere with Daniel in the hospital. Luckily, the manager who ran his hotel invited me to stay on, after Daniel had given him strict instructions to treat me "like a princess." Those were the words Daniel had said as he sauntered out the door that fated morning. "Treat my girlfriend like a princess and give her anything she wants, when she wants."

It pained my heart to think of my sullen behavior before Daniel and I had gone to bed, and that I hadn't even seen him slip away that morning, that my last words to him had been, "watch out these claws could strike", the night before. It didn't feel right to be in his penthouse without him now.

Dad decided to stay on a few more days before going back to Vermont, until Will was in the clear. It was tricky for Dad—he needed to get back to work to pay for the mounting hospital bill. The insurance was fighting the claim. After all, attacking someone could not be construed as an "accident", despite the too-slippery floors. All that money Will won on Blackjack, or whatever? Gone. Ending up "lending" it to Candy and his entourage of girls, who fed him some sob story about Candy's ill mother. I should have known.

A lawyer was on the case—poor Dad was hardly sleeping for worry, not to mention how badly he felt about Daniel. Both he and Will felt horrible, Will full of remorse, mortified by what he'd done. I remembered my twenty-five thousand dollar chip—sadly, that's where the money would be going: on a goddamn hospital bill, probably.

For the first twenty-four hours, the doctors wouldn't let me anywhere near Daniel because he was in Intensive Care and I wasn't "family," but when they saw how persistent I was, and heard my story of how I was living with him, and working with him, they relented. However, they were pretty cagey about his condition, just letting me know that it was "a question of time." I wasn't in a legal position to make any decisions anyway, so they refused to discuss details with me. But the surgery, they assured me, had been a success. Except Daniel was still lying there with tubes in him, eyes closed.

IT WAS NOW DAY THREE. After I left the hospital, to go home, take a shower and get something to eat, one of the nurses called me to let me know that Daniel had snapped out of the coma and even spoken, asking for some water, but then slipped back. It killed me that I hadn't been by his side, but the fact that his brain was coherent, that he could speak—asking for a glass of water—filled me with renewed hope. But when I tried to pin the doctors down, later, and get a clear answer as to what his chances were of a hundred percent recovery, they would not commit themselves.

None of his family had appeared. I didn't know whom to call, except Pearl, and a few of his friends from New York. I needed his address book but couldn't find it amongst his things at his apartment—I guessed it was all logged into his cellphone, which must have been on him when the ambulance brought him in.

I had been right; the hospital staff did have his phone, but they wouldn't give it to me, for privacy reasons, until they noticed—something I didn't even know myself—that Daniel had a photo of me as his screensaver.

His dad was dead, and Daniel had once told me that his mom lived in Geneva. His cell had a lock on it, but when I pressed 0000, miraculously it opened. I knew how much Daniel hated pass-words—he'd told me as much—but still, I hardly expected 0000 to work.

When I called his mother, she advised me she'd come to Vegas "when she could," as if his condition was an inconvenience. My mind boggled at some people's callous behavior. What a double whammy it must have been when Daniel realized his marriage was a sham. Poor guy, his note to me about not having had faith in women made even more sense now.

I frantically looked up online anything I could find out about TBI—traumatic brain injury. The main nurse looking after him, Barbara, warmed to me and was very friendly. I had been hanging around pretty much all day, every day, lurking in the corridors, hovering around, asking questions, until she finally let me into his room. It was a strange situation to be in. I was the sister of the guy who'd put Daniel here in the first place. They couldn't be sure, at first, I wasn't some whack-job out to finish him off, smother him with a pillow, or pull out his tubes.

"I've seen patients in worse condition who've pulled through," the nurse assured me, busying herself with his bed change. "He's already woken up twice for brief periods of time, so I'm hopeful." Her ample arms jiggled as she adjusted the stark white sheets, and her smiley face lit up the pristine room, full of tulips and roses, sent by several of his work colleagues.

I nodded like an automaton. Both times that Daniel had woken up happened to be when I wasn't around. Daniel looked like a Greek statue, so handsome and chiseled, his lips curved into an-almost smile, which gave me solace; perhaps he was dreaming of something sweet. Me? Wishful thinking.

I tried to stay upbeat, send him rays of healing light, and not let my fears get in the way of his recovery. Of all people, I knew the power of my thoughts. My simple wish of wanting Daniel and Natasha to split up, had manifested in a way I had never imagined, so I was careful to force my imagination to now focus on happy thoughts and not allow it to wander into dark ominous corridors, where doors could slam shut and leave me locked up—a prisoner of my negativity.

The nurse made to leave the room, with a pile of changed sheets in her arms. "Well, Janie, I know you'll keep an eagle eye on Daniel. I'm off to check my patient in room 303."

"The horny old man? The one that grabbed your behind and proposed marriage?" I'd heard her mention this to a friend while she was on her cellphone.

She winked at me. "Patient confidentiality, I'm not allowed to discuss my patients, you know that."

I laughed. "Good luck, see you later, Barbara."

I couldn't resist surfing on my iPad again. I needed to prepare myself. I read:

Immediately following TBI, two types of effects are seen. First, brain tissue reacts

to trauma and to tissue damage, with a series of biochemical and other physiological responses. Substances that once were safely encased within the cells now flood the brain. These processes further damage and destroy brain cells, in what is called secondary cell death.

I glugged down my soda—the burn of the bubbles prickled my nose—the word "death" made me feel sick to my stomach. I read on:

As an individual regains consciousness (those with the severest injuries may never do so), a variety of neurologically based symptoms may occur: irritability, aggression and other problems. Post-traumatic amnesia (PTA) is also typically experienced when an injured person regains consciousness. PTA refers to the period when the individual feels a sense of confusion and disorientation – Where am I? What happened? – and an inability to remember recent events.

What if Daniel wouldn't be able to remember me? That was, if he even pulled through.

Stop it, Janie, of course he's going to pull through!

**As time passes, these responses typically
subside, and the brain and other body
systems again approach physiological
stability. But, unlike tissues such as bone
or muscle, the neurons in the brain do not
mend themselves. New nerves do not
grow in ways that lead to full recovery.**

I snapped my tablet shut. It was fruitless to
worry and project about the future. I needed to get
some sleep; I was driving myself crazy.

I spent the next few hours just holding Daniel's hand, squeezing it a little, hoping, in vain, he'd
squeeze it back when I asked him if he could hear
me, or if he wanted me to kiss him.

No luck.

I finally left Daniel's side to visit my other patient: Will. Dad was there, and both were laughing
and joking. Will was on the mend and would be
returning home very soon. I only wished I felt as
free-spirited. Things could have been worse,
though . . . I had to keep reminding myself that.

But however hard I tried all I felt was anger.
Anger at myself. At Will. And oh yes, let's not
forget Cal . . . the biggest sinner of us all.

In a furious fit of rage, as I strode along the

street, trying to hail a cab to take me back to Daniel's hotel, I phoned Cal. *Damn him, if it hadn't been for his ridiculous shenanigans, none of us would be in this horrific situation.*

He finally picked up his cell on the fourth try.

"You owe us all an explanation, asshole," I shot out, "and two hospital bills, and maybe a man's life!"

"What the hell are you talking about? Janie, is that you?"

"No, it's one of your blonde bimbos coming back to haunt you—one of 'Daniel Glass" conquests, except, P.S.—while you've been going around masquerading as him—the real Daniel Glass just happens to be in a fucking coma!"

"Christ, I heard something but—"

"Oh, even better! You heard he was IN A COMA and yet you didn't even get on a plane to say that you were sorry, let alone send flowers, even after he had pulled strings for you, got you that great job when he didn't have to? Jesus, Cal, I really don't think in *all my years* I have met anyone as selfish and self-absorbed and egotistical as you! And that's saying a lot, because I've worked with some real assholes."

Silence on the line.

"Cal, are you there?"

"Yes, I'm still here."

"Do you hear me? My brother got into a scuffle with Daniel, because rumor had it Daniel—yes, Daniel Glass—was fucking half of Hollywood. Oh, and Vegas too. So my sweet little brother, who has never harmed a fly in his life, and wasn't aware of his strength, sent Daniel flying to the floor, and Daniel cracked his skull open in the fall and ended up with a hematoma to the brain—internal bleeding or whatever—and it's all your fucking fault!"

I could hear sniffling down the line.

"Cal, are you crying?" Crocodile tears no doubt, to try and garner my sympathy. Ugh!

"I'm so sorry, Janie. It was a *joke*. You know, these girls are so dumb! Once I said I was Tom Cruise and the girl believed me. Another time, I even told one that I was Marlon Brando. It was a fun game, I didn't mean to hurt anyone."

"What is *wrong* with you? With your looks, you don't need to go around *pretending* you're someone else!" I realized the irony of what I just said. Pretending he was someone else was Cal's job. And I knew he obviously suffered from the same disease that riddled so many actors' souls: desperate insecurity—even the good-looking, famous ones.

I ranted on, "I guess you never did go to MIT, did you? Never studied to be a rocket scientist, or whatever they do there?"

Silence.

"I thought so. You know, Cal, you need therapy. It's one thing to tell white lies, about your age or height, or how well you can sing, or ride a horse—all actors have to do that to get the job. But what you did was *psychopathic*!"

"I know," he mumbled. "I guess I just don't feel so good in my own skin."

I heaved out the breath I didn't realize I'd been holding in. "Never mind. The damage is done."

"I fucked up, Janie. I'm sorry, what can I do to make it up?"

"Use your imagination. You obviously have one. Put it to some good." I pressed END, squashing my finger on the keypad in a rage. I felt momentarily better to have unleashed my wrath on Cal—for all of five seconds—before I slumped onto a heap on the floor and wailed my heart out.

PEARL CAME TO VISIT Daniel in the hospital. She brought white lilies.

"I'm sorry I couldn't get here sooner," she told me, "but I was in Paris."

"Thanks so much for coming," I said, greeting her with a kiss on the cheek.

She laid her designer handbag on a chair, grabbed a vase by the bed and went to the joining bathroom to fill it with water.

It was the first time I'd seen Pearl in jeans, which showed off her curves and stunning figure. She was wearing a cream silk blouse and a gorgeous pearl choker that shimmered around her neck. Her hair was pulled up into a messy chignon. Deliberately messy. The pearls were overkill, though. They belonged with a ball gown, not with jeans.

Pearl looked down at Daniel, a tender smile passed across her face. "I brought my iPod full of my favorite songs for Daniel to listen to—it may help. Don't lose hope, Janie, I was in a coma and a lot of people didn't believe I'd come out of it."

"You were in a *coma*? Really?"

"Would you believe it, I was listening to 'Wake Up Little Suzy' when I finally came to."

It was a brilliant idea to bring Daniel songs, why hadn't I thought of that? "Great gift," I said, "thank you so much. How long ago were you in a coma? What happened"

"A few years ago. Like Daniel, it was a silly accident. It's usually that way. Go skydiving and you're fine, walk down some steps too fast, with the wrong shoes on, and boom, your life changes in seconds. Leather soled shoes can be lethal. I noticed Daniel favors elegant shoes."

Pearl had been in a coma? Hope washed over me like the seventh wave. "How long did it take you to recover?"

"I was out for . . . I think it was three days. You know, I can't remember a thing, but for my family it felt like a lifetime. My brother had overheard some of the neurologists discussing a patient, saying that person was brain dead, and Anthony thought they were talking about me. It was high drama for a while, but I pulled through."

"Luck was on your side," I said.

"Talking of luck, Janie, I've brought something I believe is blessed with special lucky powers. Every time I wear it, miracles happen. I thought I'd lend it to Daniel until he gets better." She hooked her hands around her neck. "Actually, can you help me unclasp it?" She turned her back to me and brushed some loose blond tendrils of hair from the nape of her neck.

"Sure." I fumbled with the diamond clasp, set in an intricate pattern. This was one hell of a necklace—it must have cost a fortune.

"This choker was a gift from my husband," she let me know. "It's genuine Art Deco and belonged to a famous socialite in Paris who was a great beauty in her day. There are eighty-eight pearls. Did you know that 88 is the number of infinity? There's no ending with a number eight, no beginning, it just keeps going on and on. Eighty-eight is a magical number; there are eighty-eight keys on a piano, it's the number of days that Mercury takes to revolve around the sun. Isn't that interesting?"

Finally, I managed to unhook the clasp. The heavy pearls plopped into my hands, smooth and glimmering and catching prisms of light. It seemed there were a thousand colors in these gems: pinks and honey tones. Pearl's generosity was overwhelming—the pearls looked so valuable, but I wasn't about to make a fuss, Daniel needed all the luck he could get. And I, being superstitious, believed the necklace was lucky. Why not? It had been proven by scientists that even inanimate objects had a life of their own.

Pearl went on, "Daniel doesn't have to wear them on his neck—God forbid, the doctors probably wouldn't even let him—but you know, you can let them touch his skin, nestle them by his shoulders or under his neck. We'll tell the nurse and doctors so they don't think they're some cheap trinket from a Jack in-the-box and throw them out."

"Are you sure? You're okay *leaving* them here?"

"These pearls are very, very precious to me, but if they can save a man's life . . . look, maybe you think I'm a little crazy, but I believe in lucky charms, and I know how much Daniel means to you."

"You do?"

Pearl smiled. "Janie, I know true love when I see it. And with you two, it isn't just one-sided, either. I could tell in that meeting—in both meetings in fact, how crazy he is about you."

My stomach fluttered, remembering that mad kiss when I straddled Daniel in front of Pearl. I held the pearls in both hands, still amazed at her kindness. Most people this wealthy didn't have a heart like Pearl's. My eyes smarted with tears.

"You really think he has a chance?" I murmured, wiping a tear from my cheek.

"I know he does. I'm living proof."

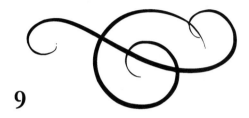

9

DAY FOUR. I GOT TO the hospital very early, with a bundle of poetry books under my arm that I found at Daniel's apartment. I'd been reading so many stories online of ex coma patients who said that while they were completely immobile in a coma, their brains were active and aware of everything going on around them, down to conversations between families and their doctors. "Frustration," one wrote, "didn't even begin to describe how I felt." Their brains were lucid, even, in some cases, when they had been pronounced "brain dead." I thought of Natasha and had to wonder.

Daniel lay there, covered in crisp, starched, hospital sheets. I checked for the pearls that Barbara had promised would be safe. They were nestled along the side of Daniel's torso. He looked beautiful; they had combed back his dark hair, and his fine cheekbones and beautiful bone structure reminded me of what he once said about his ancestry: a dash of Native American blood ran through his veins. With his lids shut, it was disarming not being able to see his magical blue eyes that were so much a part of his personality. I imagined him just sleeping—not in a coma at all—and decided that he could hear everything I was saying.

"Hey, gorgeous." I leaned down and kissed him, resting my head on the planes of his face, breathing in the Daniel scent that even the nurse, the medications, and the hospital surroundings hadn't managed to erase. "I love you," I whispered into his ear. "I know you can hear me, I know you're going to get better. You're just taking a nap, which is fine, but you know, I'm ready for you to wake up now. We all are. We have a movie to make, after all."

I began to gently massage his shoulders—something the nurse told me was very important so the muscles didn't atrophy. I nuzzled my nose into his neck while I did so, kneaded his biceps, his forearms—the muscles like taut ropes— remembering so clearly what it was like to have those arms wrapped tightly around my body. But I refused to cry. Refused to give in. *He will get better! He has to!*

I went to the bathroom adjoining his room, peed, washed my hands, and when I came back into the room, I swear he opened an eye.

"What's that squeaking sound?" Daniel mumbled. He was alive and talking! He'd heard my sneakers squeaking on the polished floor.

I raced to his bedside, my heart thundering through my chest and out the other side. I leaned over him, too scared to touch his face for fear of hurting him.

He opened the other eye. "Wow, who do we have here?"

Tears misted my vision. Tears of gratitude. The doctors had told me that, so far, there was no sign of brain damage, but this I hadn't imagined! Daniel talking normally! I leaned over him and laid my lips on his, breathed him in, and planted a sweet kiss there.

"Beautiful angel," he whispered, "am I hallucinating? Kiss me, kiss me and show me you're real."

I started tentatively, little kisses all over his jaw, his chin, the edges of his sculpted mouth, but he caught my lip between his teeth and groaned. He could hardly move, though, and was very much the invalid. I cupped his head gently in my hands, terrified of pressing too hard, but steadied him as I deepened the kiss, my tongue meeting his, and they tangled together in relief, in ecstasy, our tastes mingling into one. I moaned into him.

I murmured, "Daniel, I need to get the nurse. Need to let them know you've woken up."

But he interrupted my better sense of judgment. "Don't you dare, I want to savor this moment with you, and you alone." His tongue found mine again, his kiss laced with lust.

"Good," he growled, "I can feel it's all working down there."

"What is?"

"Pull the sheet off and see for yourself."

My gaze wandered to the middle of his body. The sheet was tented. Contrary to what the medics said could happen—that Daniel would lose his libido—his erection was alive and well! A huge grin spread across my face. I peeled the sheet back and there it was: that beautiful part of Daniel's anatomy that still had me having wet dreams every night. I gasped. Even my dreams had betrayed me: Daniel's cock was more glorious than any fantasy. Smooth. Huge. His wide crest throbbing with anticipation.

"Lick it, suck it, fuck my cock with your mouth."

Ever the dirty talk. That hadn't changed. "Am I allowed to do this?" I said. "Isn't it . . . I don't know . . . *dangerous* in some way? Shouldn't I let them know you've come out of your coma?"

"Don't be disobedient, just wrap your lips around my cock."

Did he even recognize me? He didn't call me by name. But his sexy voice, and seeing him all in one piece, flooded my body with a nervous thrill. If I was a stranger to him, never mind, he still wanted me. My nipples peaked, my panties suddenly sticky with that familiar rush of liquid heat pooling between my legs. I looked around the room and perked up my ears like a dog. Silence, the coast was clear—nurses were on their coffee breaks.

"Do as I say," he growled.

I laid the sheet aside to give myself full view of the totality of Daniel's beauty. His cock rose up to his navel, sprinkled with a line of fine hair that skittered up to his wide chest. His nipples were flat and hard, his pectorals defined but not bulky, his golden skin stretched taut—not an inch of fat anywhere.

"Suck it, make me come in your sexy mouth," he commanded in a low but quiet voice, almost a whisper.

I took his balls gently in my hand, bent my head down and licked him up and down, then widened my mouth over each one in turn, sucking them with relish.

"Oh fuck, you sexy girl." He tried to flex his hips toward me, but only managed a twitch. There were golden and black bruises on the side of his left thigh, the point where he must have fallen.

I trailed my tongue up his solid length, aware of the throbbing veins pulsing out to the max, eager for my touch, desperate for release after all this time bed-bound. I licked the underside up and down, while squeezing him tightly in my fist at the tip. He groaned loudly. I moved around the bed to better position myself, my back to his face so I could feed my hungry mouth with all of him, stuffing his huge cock right to the back of my throat until I gagged, and even then he was too big for me.

"I love you," he moaned. "I'm going to fuck you so hard, fuck you all day and all night when I'm better. Christ, baby you're driving me wild."

Still no mention of my name. I started pumping him with my mouth, tight as a fitted glove, enveloping my lips around his cock like a vice. I held the base of him, squeezing, tensing my grip, pumping him back and forth. Every now and then I'd take his huge erection out of my mouth and flicker my tongue around his peephole, which was thick with creamy arousal, and circle his throbbing crown around and around. Alternating the rhythm—pumping one moment and teasing the next—I had Daniel in a state of fever, growling and cursing, his thick girth expanding and threatening any second to explode into my mouth.

"Your hot wet juicy cunt is going to get so fucked by me soon. I'm going to take you and thrust myself in so hard—come so fucking hard in your tight pussy . . . aaah! Fuck, baby . . . Christ . . . I'm . . . I'm coming!" His scalding seed, so much of it, fired out massive spurts to the back of my throat. I swallowed several times, so fast and furiously it came shooting out. I was so turned on, I took my hands away and rubbed them vigorously between my legs. It didn't take much for my orgasm—spurned on by Daniel's dirty talk—to pound through me.

A few minutes later, when his groans had waned, he let out a chuckle of laughter.

"What?" I said.

"That was great but . . . what's your name again?"

I froze. Question answered: he didn't recognize me.

"Janie," I whispered, placing the sheet over him. I didn't need to clean him up I'd swallowed every drop, licked him spotless. I could hear voices: chatter getting nearer to the room. I stood up to attention, as if we were innocently discussing the weather or something.

Daniel winked at me, a grin stretched across his face. "I missed you, baby."

"I thought you didn't know who I was." Perhaps he'd been kidding all along. My heart was racing with nerves, excitement, and fear. I'd been through so much the last few days while he had been in dreamland, oblivious to the agony I'd been through—to him, I supposed, it was like minutes, not days—and now he was free to feel jovial and amused. I, on the other hand, was still reeling in shock, terrified he'd slip away again.

"Please don't ever do that to me again," I murmured on a breath into his ear, "I thought I'd die of misery."

"It was a one-off," he joked. That was the very phrase I'd used, just the other night. "By the way," he said in a rasp, "I have a favor to ask."

"Anything," I said.

"Anything?"

"Anything," I assured him.

"Marry me, Janie." He closed his eyes, as if exhausted by the energy expended with my blowjob, but his lips curved into a satisfied, content smile.

As if a tornado had struck, the door flew open in a gust, interrupting our peace, and in came a team of doctors. I glanced at Daniel, but his eyes were still shut, unfazed by the commotion and loud chatter around him.

I looked up. A smiling face I'd seen a hundred times online, in magazines, and even on stage, gazed at me. She was different in the flesh. Not as tall, her hair a shade or two darker, her bust less ample. Vomit rose to my throat, I thought I'd faint again. *I am seeing things, hallucinating, I must be!*

Because there was no way this could be real:

Natasha freaking Jürgen!

I DIDN'T FAINT, but I did collapse onto the floor, my knees like Jell-O. They fussed around Daniel. It sounded as if they were administering extra medication. Their talk was white noise buzzing in my ears. Then the woman spoke louder:

"Get her some water. I've heard the poor thing hasn't been sleeping, has been hanging out here almost 24/7."

Hanging out? Was she referring to me?

I looked up, my vision a haze. But it was her. It was Natasha Jürgen. I wasn't dreaming because I pinched myself. My faculties were all there.

"What are you doing here?" I croaked out, my throat drier than chalk.

"You must be Janie, right? The nurses have told me all about you."

I felt another rise of bile threatening to spill all over the floor. But my legs were too weak to move.

She leaned down and held out her hand to shake mine. "I'm Kristin, Daniel's new doctor."

"But you look like—"

She handed me a glass of water. "I know, I know." She laughed, her gleaming teeth so white they matched the hospital sheets.

"Who *are* you?" I managed, wondering why Daniel wasn't saying anything; maybe the drugs they'd just given him were making him woozy. I glugged the water down but my throat still felt dry. My tongue was so thick in my mouth I could hardly get my words out.

"I'm Daniel's sister-in-law, Kristin. Natasha's sister. I'm a neurologist, you know, highly trained and experienced in all things to do with traumatic brain injury; it's my specialty. Here, let me help you up off the floor." She pulled me up, my sneakers squeaking again on the linoleum.

This wasn't right!

"His new doctor?" My voice was barely a squeak. "Where's Dr. Bellow?"

"Dr. Bellow has been transferred to another hospital, to another state. I'll be handling Daniel's case from now on. Who better than his very own sister-in-law, after all?" She smiled at me again. All sweetness and light. On second glance, I saw that she *was* different from Natasha. Her mouth less lush, her lips harder. Her eyes more feline, too. And she looked several years older than Natasha. But still, they were so alike it was uncanny.

I turned my attention to Daniel. "Daniel, baby, Kristin's here." I squeezed his hand. He didn't flinch, and his eyes remained closed.

"He can't hear you," she said coolly, snapping her pen into her clipboard. "He may never come out of this, you need to be prepared, Janie."

"He's just sleeping," I assured her. "He was awake just five minutes ago, before you all came in."

The other doctor, a slim young man, whom I'd never seen before, prized open Daniel's lids and shone a light pen in his eyes. "No, he's out cold," he confirmed. "The patient is in a full coma."

"He was awake! I swear it!" I cried. "Just before you came into the room we . . . we were talking and joking and we . . . we . . . " I broke off, stunned.

Natasha Jürgen's sister looked into my eyes, a pitiful gaze that told me how sorry she felt for me.

"Janie, I can give you something, you know. A sedative, something to help you relax, take away the anxiety, take away some of the pain."

"What is wrong with you all? He was *talking* to me! More than talking!" I didn't want to get into details about the blowjob. "You have to believe me. The nurse . . . Barbara . . . where is she? She'll tell you . . . Daniel has already snapped out of the coma twice, but slipped back again! But he's on the mend!"

"Nurse Mendez is on leave—she won't be back for a long while. And I can assure you, there is no evidence of lucidity in Daniel's medical file. No notes to that effect."

"What?" I screeched. "This is *insane*! Where are all the doctors who know what's going on? Daniel is pulling through. Daniel is—"

"Calm down, Janie." Kristin clinched me by the crook of my arm. "I know this is hard to accept, but Daniel—to put in layman's terms so you'll understand—has brain damage from internal bleeding, which resulted in a lack of oxygen to the brain. I have studied his case in depth—unless a miracle happens, he will never recover."

"No, no, that's not what the nurse told me!

And if that were true he wouldn't have been able to communicate. He was speaking! There is nothing wrong with him!" I started to shake Daniel vigorously. "Daniel, Daniel, baby, wake up! Tell them you were talking to me! Tell them what happened!" But he wasn't responding. I turned to the doctors. "He was awake just five minutes ago, what did you just give him? He was awake!"

She shook her head.

"Why won't you believe me?" I bellowed. "We kissed, we did more, he just had an orgasm, you can check for yourself, we—"

"Give her a shot, she's out of control." Kristin's voice was cool but stern. Unemotional. Calculating. Nurse Ratched in *One Flew Over the Cuckoo's Nest*. "She needs to calm the hell down. We can't have this kind of commotion going on. Prepare the syringe, I'll hold her."

I started thrashing, yelling and screaming. "Let me go! You have no legal right to do this! Let me go! What the hell are you doing? Let me g—" I could feel the needle sliding into my vein.

And then I blanked out.

I WOKE UP several hours later, according to the

time on my watch. My head hurt, I ached—I felt like I'd run a marathon, or was just recovering from a bout of heavy flu. Then I remembered. I jolted up and rubbed my eyes. That bitch!

I was still in Daniel's room, lying on a reclining chair. Everything was the same: the vase of lilies Pearl had brought, the roses Star had sent. But Daniel wasn't there! My eyes roamed around the room frantically: they'd taken him away! I jumped up from the chair and raced to the phone on Daniel's bedside table. Not "bedside" anymore because there was no bed—they'd wheeled him out of here. I dialed the extension where the nurses' station was.

A bright voice picked up.

"Where's Daniel Glass?" I demanded. "He was here, in Room 313, but now he's vanished!"

"Just a moment I'll look at my chart. And you are?"

"His fiancée," I said. I *was* his fiancée—he'd proposed to me—and no, I hadn't been dreaming.

"He's been transferred," she told me.

My pulse was thundering in my head, in my stomach, my heart; so much so, I thought I'd black out again. I needed to eat something. "Where?"

"I'm sorry, I do not have that information at this time."

"Don't have it, or won't give it?"

"I do not have that information, ma'am, you'll have to speak to his doctor."

"Dr. Bellows?" I said hopefully.

"No, ma'am, Dr. Bellows left us yesterday. He is no longer working at this hospital. Dr. Jürgen is in charge of Mr. Glass' case—you'll need to speak to her."

"Can you tell me where Dr. Bellows has been transferred to?"

"I'm sorry, I do not have that information at this time."

"What about the nurse who was looking after him? Barbara. I think her last name is Mendez. Can you tell me where she has gone?"

"I believe she is on leave."

"How can I contact her? Do you have her phone number? Address?" I didn't need to hear her answer; I knew what it would be.

"I'm sorry, ma'am, I do not—"

"Have that information at this time," I finished off. "At this time? Or any time? How can I find out?" I begged, my voice a desperate plea.

"I'm sure Dr. Jürgen will be most helpful, she's a very respected neurologist; we're lucky to have her with us. I can arrange an appointment with her tomorrow, if you wish."

"That won't be necessary, thank you."

I tried to put down the receiver but my hands were trembling so badly, I didn't manage to get it on its cradle. I needed back up. It was dangerous for me here. What Kristin Jürgen did to me was unethical, illegal, and insane, but she was in her own environment, a star in her neurological world, obviously. Doctors were bad enough at the best of times—always backing each other up, even when it came to malpractice. I could sue the bitch for what she did to me, I thought, for what *she was doing now* to Daniel . . . whatever, I needed to get away from here and organize backup, not be here alone. I glugged down an entire glass of water, grabbed my purse, then made for the door, half expecting it to be locked. It wasn't.

I wanted to run around the hospital, screaming for Daniel, demanding his whereabouts, but I knew that would be crazy: I'd end up sedated again. No, I needed to come back, armed with an attorney, and maybe even a police officer. Somehow, I had to find another expert, another neurologist who could offer a second opinion about Daniel's condition. Subpoena Dr. Bellows, Barbara, and all the original medical notes they took. Whatever was going on was ominous, like something out of a psychological horror movie.

This Kristen Jürgen was a coldhearted, scheming bitch and, for some strange reason, she wanted Daniel to stay in his coma.

A light bulb flashed in my brain . . . duh, *how could I be so slow on the uptake?*

Natasha Jürgen didn't come out of her coma, either. A coincidence?

I don't think so.

I HAILED A CAB and started to dial the numbers of everyone I knew, starting with Pearl, kicking myself that I had never asked for the nurse's personal cellphone number. With all Pearl's contacts and her husband's money, they were bound to know the most powerful attorneys in the country. Not to mention the fact I needed to let her know that her pearl necklace had vanished along with Daniel. Her phone went to voicemail. Then I called Star. Damn voicemail. I left a frantic message. And when I finally tracked down Pearl's PA, she told me that she and her husband were on their "no email, no cellphone vacation."

"What do you mean?" I asked, bewildered. Who went without their cellphone these days? Apparently they did. For two whole weeks a year, Alexandre Chevalier had a no contact rule, except for direct members of family, his dogs, or if one of his houses was burning down, strict instructions not to be disturbed. The PA gave me numbers of all their lawyers, but Star had once told me that Alexandre Chevalier had "underground methods," to deal with "severe problems"—her kidnapping, I remembered Star telling me, was solved in part because of him.

I thought of Daniel's marriage proposal just a few hours earlier, and wondered if he was aware of what he was doing. For that short minute, before Kristin psycho Jürgen and her team entered the room, I entertained images of our future together: walking down Fifth Avenue, arm in arm, maybe ice skating in Central Park, the lake frozen in winter, or diving into glittering turquoise waters in the Mediterranean on his island hideaway in Hydra. Me pregnant, maybe. Collaborating on plays, always the husband and wife team; an everlasting marriage, growing old and gray together.

And now, all this seemed impossible.

I paid the cab driver and made my way through the revolving doors to Daniel's apartment. I needed to shower and change, and cash in that $25,000 Bellagio chip. I walked into the shiny marble lobby, forever fearful now about too-polished floors. Daniel never kept a key for his apartment, because there was a twenty-four hour concierge.

"Hi, Ethan," I said, my elbows plunked on the counter, as I waited for him to give me the key to the suite. I expected him to ask after "Mr. Glass" as they always did, but he stared at me, his face unsmiling, his stance brisk.

"May I help you?"

"Hi Ethan," I said, ignoring his rudeness, "I need the key please. I'm pooped!"

"I'm afraid I'm not at liberty to let you up there, Miss Cole."

Miss Cole? What the hell was going on? "Ethan! My stuff is up there. I need a shower, something to eat. You know Daniel wanted me to be here. He told you to give me anything I needed. And right now, I need a shower!"

"Just one moment."

"Thank you," I said, still stunned by his suddenly cold behavior. But he didn't give me the room key. He bent down, picked up a suitcase and wheeled it out from behind the desk. My suitcase!

"Your things have been packed, Miss."

"Miss? My name is Janie! What the heck is this? Why are you suddenly not letting me into Daniel's apartment?"

"Just following orders. I'm sorry, this is out of my control."

"Whose orders?"

"My boss."

"Your boss?"

"The person who owns this hotel."

At first: confusion. Then: delight. I got it now! The reason Daniel hadn't been in his room in the hospital was that he had recovered! And he'd spoken to Ethan. But why didn't Daniel want me to stay? Maybe he was planning a surprise for me.

"You've spoken to Daniel? Like, recently?" I asked.

"No, I believe he's still ill, isn't he? Still in the hospital?"

This was surreal. "You said just now, 'your boss'."

"Mrs. Glass."

"His *mom* is here? She arrived from Geneva already?"

"No, not his mother."

"But you just said 'Mrs. Glass'."

"Yes, Mrs. Glass. The wife of Daniel Glass."

"But his wife died last year."

"I wouldn't know about his late wife, miss, I've only been working for Mr. Glass for four months."

Blood was pounding in my ears. I felt faint. Weak. I hadn't eaten properly, not taken my iron pills or had a proper hot meal in days, and whatever drug I'd been injected with was making me feel hung over and dizzy. My hands and legs were trembling; I could hardly stand. I leaned against the desk for fear of falling.

"What's his wife's name?" I croaked out, somehow knowing what the dreaded answer would be before Ethan even opened his mouth.

"Her first name is Kristin. I believe her name before she married was Jürgen."

TO BE CONTINUED . . . .

The final part of this trilogy, *Hearts of Glass*, will be released in April/May 2015. Please join my mailing list or join me on Facebook to be informed of its release date and any other future releases.

Thank you so much for choosing **Broken Glass** to be part of your library and I hope you enjoyed reading it as much as I enjoyed writing it. If you loved this book and have a minute please write a quick review. It helps authors so much. I am thrilled that you chose my book to be part of your busy life and hope to be re-invited to your bookshelf with my next release.

If you haven't read my other books I would love you to give them a try. The Pearl Series is a set of five, full-length erotic romance novels. If you'd like to know more about Star and Jake, you can read their story in *The Star Trilogy*. I have also written a suspense novel, *Stolen Grace*.

The Pearl Trilogy
(all three books in one big volume)

Shades of Pearl
Shadows of Pearl
Shimmers of Pearl
Pearl
Belle Pearl

The Star Trilogy
Stolen Grace
Shards of Glass

Join me on Facebook
(facebook.com/AuthorArianneRichmonde)

Join me on Twitter
(@A_Richmonde)

For more information about me, visit my website
(www.ariannerichmonde.com).

If you would like to email me:
ariannerichmonde@gmail.com

Made in the USA
San Bernardino, CA
23 September 2016